PRAISE FOR *WHAT LIVES IN THE WOODS*

"Currie throws all the frightfully fun trappings of haunted-house tales at readers, who will soak up the stormy nights, town rumors, exploding light bulbs, creeping shadows, unsettling whispers...light horror for larger collections."

—*Booklist*

PRAISE FOR LINDSAY CURRIE

"A teeth-chattering, eyes bulging, shuddering-and-shaking, chills-at-the-back-of-your-neck ghost story. I loved it!"

—R. L. Stine, author of the Goosebumps series on *Scritch Scratch*

"A spine-tingling blend of hauntings and history."

—*Publishers Weekly* on *Scritch Scratch*

"*Scritch Scratch* brims with eerie thrills and nail-biting chills that are sure to keep readers turning pages. Don't dare read this at night!"

—Kate Hannigan, author of the League of Secret Heroes series on *Scritch Scratch*

"Delightfully chilling and rooted in history, this haunting thrill ride will keep you hooked."

—Jess Keating, author of *Nikki Tesla and the Ferret-Proof Death Ray* on *Scritch Scratch*

"Mary Downing Hahn fans will enjoy this just-right blend of history and spooky."
—*Kirkus Reviews* on *Scritch Scratch*

"[A] scary tale that lives up to the reputation of haunted Chicago...offers a ghost-hunterly blend of reality and chills that should appeal to many readers with creepy interests."
—*Bulletin of the Center for Children's Books* on *Scritch Scratch*

"Delightfully chilling and rooted in history, this haunting thrill ride will keep you hooked."
—Jarrett Lerner, author of the EngiNerds series on *Scritch Scratch*

"Give this page-turner to readers seeking a spooky thrill reminiscent of books by Mary Downing Hahn and filled with strong family relationships, budding friendships, a local history, mystery, and creepiness."
—*School Library Journal* on *The Peculiar Incident on Shady Street*

"Shivers aplenty; just the ticket for a cold autumn night."
—*Kirkus Reviews* on *The Peculiar Incident on Shady Street*

"A perfect flashlight read, Currie's debut is peppered with incidents that will make the reader's skin crawl and teeth chatter."
—*Booklist* on *The Peculiar Incident on Shady Street*

ALSO BY LINDSAY CURRIE

Scritch Scratch

The Peculiar Incident on Shady Street

WHAT LIVES IN THE WOODS

LINDSAY CURRIE

sourcebooks
young readers

Published by Sourcebooks Young Readers, an imprint of Sourcebooks Kids
P.O. Box 4410, Naperville, Illinois 60567-4410
(630) 961-3900
sourcebookskids.com

Library of Congress Cataloging-in-Publication data is on file with the publisher.

Source of Production: Sheridan Books, Chelsea, Michigan, United States
Date of Production: July 2022
Run Number: 5027305

Printed and bound in the United States of America.
SB 10 9 8 7 6 5 4 3

To John, Rob, Ben, and Ella.
Thank you for sending me on the writing
retreat that sparked this book.
You're the best!

CHAPTER ONE

"We're going where?" Leo exclaims, spraying bits of pretzel from his mouth onto Mom's favorite rug.

Dad winces, then reaches out and gently puts his plate down on the table. I smother my laugh, thinking that he looks like a zookeeper cautiously feeding a lion. Except Leo wouldn't be a lion. He'd be...I don't know...a wild pig, maybe?

"We're going to Saugatuck," Dad finally answers with a flourish. "It's in Michigan."

"You guys will love it!" Mom peeks through the kitchen door and gives a reassuring smile. Her hair is held back by a red bandanna and her cheeks are a splotchy pink, probably from the heat of the oven. Mom's never liked to cook, but lately she's trying to change that. Mom says learning to bake is her new resolution, even though it's the summer. Unfortunately, her new resolution is off to a rocky start. Yesterday she baked a tray of charred cookies. And last week she served homemade bread that tasted (and smelled) like someone put Leo's gym socks in the oven. I think she just needs a distraction from her busy tutoring business but *wow*. "Saugatuck is a quaint little town on Lake Michigan."

Leo's eyebrows knit together in confusion. "But *Chicago* is on Lake Michigan. Why would we go to Michigan for the lake when we can walk a few blocks and see it right here?"

Dad chuckles. "Fair enough, but Saugatuck is a little more than two hours away and very different. It'll be a pleasant getaway for us this summer. Nice shops, galleries..." He eyes Leo's pretzel. "And restaurants! Plenty of those." He swivels his head toward me. "Haven't heard anything from you yet, Gin. What are you thinking?"

Good question. Truth is, I haven't said anything about this idea because I'm not sure what to think yet. I like the idea of a vacation, but this seems...sudden?

"Ginny?" Dad prompts, looking concerned. "You okay?"

I nod. "Mm-hmm. Just wondering when we're leaving."

"In three days," Dad answers.

Three days would be Saturday. Still seems sudden, but at least I have time to pack. "Okay. So, we're gone for the weekend then?"

He hesitates a moment too long before finally saying, "Yes and no. We're actually going to be gone for a month."

"A month?" Leo and I shout in unison. We've never gone anywhere for a month! In fact, since Dad is a restoration expert, he's always busy researching and fixing up old buildings in Chicago, so we hardly go anywhere at all. Between his clients and Mom's students, it's basically impossible to leave.

It *would* be nice for once, though. Mom and Dad both seem excited about this place. Maybe it could be a good thing. Except...

"Wait! What about my writing class? It starts in a week. If we're gone for a month, I'll miss most of it."

Dad exchanges a somber look with Mom. "We need to talk to you about that, honey. There's another class starting in September. We'll need to switch you into that one."

"September?" I squeak out. By then, I'll be in eighth grade. School will be in session, so I'll have homework. Field hockey. Choir. I'll be too busy to go to a class two nights a week no matter how much I want to. "I can't go in September!"

Dad lifts his hands up, palms facing me surrender-style. "I'm sorry. I know this isn't ideal, but this trip is a good opportunity. We can't turn it down."

I'm speechless. I've been signed up for the Mystery

3

Writing Workshop with my best friend, Erica, for weeks. Nothing that makes me give that up is a good opportunity.

"And I know a month sounds like a long time, but you'll be glad once you see it. We're not just staying in a little place on the lake. We're staying in a *mansion*." He places extra emphasis on the word *mansion*. "It's called Woodmoor Manor, and it has twenty-six rooms! Imagine having that much space all to ourselves. You could practically write in a new room every day!"

I smile weakly at his room-hopping idea. But twenty-six rooms and we're the only guests? That seems weird. "What is it? I mean, is it a hotel or a bed-and-breakfast?"

"It's neither," Dad says with a lopsided grin. "It's technically not a resort, but I pulled a few strings and got permission for us to stay there."

I narrow my eyes. If this were a mystery novel, this would be the moment I realize someone is either lying or covering up the truth. Things don't add up.

"If it isn't a resort or a hotel or an inn, then what is it?" I ask.

"It's kind of a museum," he answers. "Woodmoor was built in the nineteen thirties by a millionaire from Chicago."

"We're staying in a *museum*?" The more Dad talks, the fishier this sounds. I lean over and elbow my brother in the ribs, then widen my eyes at him. He gets my drift and stops picking salt off his pretzel to refocus on Dad.

"We are." Dad slides a picture in front of us. It's a sprawling brick building that looks like it's sitting on a hill. "People love seeing old buildings restored to their original beauty, and I'm definitely up for the challenge on this one!"

Ugh. I knew it! This isn't a vacation. It's another one of Dad's projects. I may not totally understand his job, but I understand enough. He studies the history of different buildings so they can be fixed up the way they were meant to look originally. That means pretty much everything he works on is old. And most of the time, old equals run-down.

I glance back at the picture. I bet this mansion is a mess. Dark and cold with cobwebs in every corner. I'm going to miss my workshop for *this*?

"But is there a gym there? How will I practice and run drills?"

"You can go one month without basketball, Leo," my mother's voice echoes in from the kitchen. "We need a break from our schedules anyway. It's too hectic around here."

I can't believe this. Why are we changing around our entire summer for just one job?

Because the owners are paying Dad a lot. This mansion could be like the hotel he helped renovate a few years ago. It was old and shabby and the owners said they were going to go out of business if something didn't change. Dad took the job and now he says it's always booked and almost as popular as some of the famous hotels. The hotel people were desperate. Bad desperate. The people in Michigan must be desperate too. The question is, why?

"Is there a lot of stuff wrong with the mansion?" I ask. "Like is it falling down or covered in mold or something?"

Dad opens his mouth, then promptly shuts it again. Mom peeks back through the kitchen door, her expression suddenly more "oh, no" than "yay, vacation."

Uh-oh.

"Not wrong with it, no," Dad starts, his tone unsettling. "It's just that the owners would like to start using it as an event space. You know, host weddings and other large parties there. They want me to come in and find ways to spruce up the place a bit, make it a little more...*welcoming*. But historically accurate, of course."

I fold my arms over my chest. "If it's as big and awesome as you say it is, wouldn't that be easy? People would want to book events there, right?"

"Well, it's not exactly set up for that right now. Plus, there *might* be some rumors about it."

"What kind of rumors?" I ask, a chill sliding up my spine.

"Nothing for you guys to worry about. All you need to

know is that the town is nice, Woodmoor is beautiful, and our summer is going to be incredible."

Well, that settles it. He's definitely hiding something. I try to brush off the goose bumps forming on my arms, but they won't budge. The rumors about the mansion are bad. They have to be. If the owners are desperate like the owners of the hotel were, then there's a serious problem they want Dad to fix.

Maybe someone died there. Or maybe more than one person! Maybe all the museum people got food poisoning, or a bear broke in and killed them all! Wait, do they even have bears in Michigan?

I drop my head into my hands, horrible thoughts swimming around in my brain. This is why I am going to be a writer someday, like Agatha Christie. I didn't even know who she was until earlier this year when my whole grade had to read one of her books for English. It. Was. Amazing. Since then, I've read as many as I can. I also decided I'm going to write mysteries someday too. My imagination just never turns off.

"Looks like we're gonna be staying in a haunted house," Leo says with a chuckle. "Perfect for you, right, Nancy Drew?"

I shove him and groan. This Michigan trip means Erica will probably take the workshop without me. Even if I can take it in September, I'll be alone then. And now I find out we'll be stuck in a crumbling, old mansion for four whole weeks? No way. If Dad is planning to spend half the summer in Michigan, then he'll have to do it without me. I am one hundred percent, absolutely, positively *not* going.

CHAPTER TWO

Three Days Later
Saugatuck, Michigan

"Thought you weren't going," Leo mocks.

"Shut up," I snap, stretching out my legs as far as our cramped minivan will allow. When Dad said Saugatuck was a little more than two hours away, he must have forgotten about traffic, because we've been in the car for over three. Add in the one-hour time difference, and it's after three o'clock already. "You could have had my back about this whole thing, you know."

"Chill out, Gin," Leo says, tossing his basketball from one hand to another. "You're being a baby. It's not gonna be that bad."

I shake my head. My brother can be really dense sometimes. He's eighteen months older than me, and you'd think that would make him wiser, but no. It only makes him bigger and smellier. "Whatever. Just don't come crawling to me when you finally realize Dad is moving us into some leaky old building with asbestos in the walls."

"How do you know it's leaky or has asbestos?" he asks, then laughs when I scrunch up my face. "Oh, right. You don't." He's quiet for a moment before asking, "What's asbestos?"

"Never mind the asbestos." I angle myself so I'm facing him. "And since when are you Mr. Positivity, anyway? You're going to be there with no basketball and no friends. For a *month!*"

My brother waves me off. "Yeah, yeah. I know. But there's two public basketball courts in Saugatuck. Mom said she'll drive me over there anytime. I'll be able to pick up some games with people around there for sure."

He pauses and gives me one of his looks I hate so much. The one where he's trying to act like an adult even though he's only fourteen. "I think you're being extra annoying about all this because you wanted to go somewhere fancy. Well, we aren't. So, get over it."

I huff and sink back down into my seat. Of course, that's what my brother would think is wrong with me. He pays less attention to me than he does his homework. But I expected more from my parents. I thought they knew how much the writing workshop meant to me. Guess I was wrong.

"Hey," Leo says, nudging me. "Don't you want one of those old typing machines?"

"You mean a typewriter?" I ask, fighting off a laugh. "What's that have to do with it?"

He rolls his eyes at me. "I think I just saw one in the window of that antique store back there. You were too busy pouting to notice."

"What?" I crane my neck and plant my palms on the window, but it's too late. The shop is too far behind us. "You're sure it was a typewriter?"

"I know what they look like, Gin. You should buy it," he says, laughing. "You already read weird old books. If you get that typewriter, you can do your homework on a weird old machine too."

"Agatha Christie's books are not weird! If you'd try reading something other than potato chip bags, you'd know that!" The typewriter I've been dreaming of for months pops into my mind. It's black and shiny and so perfect. I can imagine myself sitting at it, plinking out the next bestseller just like Agatha would have. Of course, without the writing workshop, I'm going to be teaching myself this summer.

Dad pulls into a parking spot. I sneak a glance at him in the rearview mirror as he unbuckles his seat belt. His eyes meet mine. "You aren't still mad at me, are you?"

"Not mad. Just disappointed."

He sighs. It's long and drawn out, like he's just heard the worst news possible. "Please don't be. Just give it a chance, okay?"

I clench my hands together in my lap until my knuckles are white. "What about the rumors? The *legends*. Am I supposed to give those a chance too?"

The car goes silent. Up until now, Mom and Dad had no idea I've done my own research into Woodmoor. But a good mystery writer *always* researches.

Dad closes his car door, then opens mine. His expression is serious. "Okay, Sherlock. Spill it. What have you dug up now?"

"Oh, just that everyone here believes mutant creatures live in the woods around the mansion."

Hitchhikers. That's what the locals call the creatures with large heads they swear prowl around the woods that surround the mansion. Rumor has it a mad scientist was performing horrible experiments on people a hundred years ago, and they became these twisted-up creatures. One day the creatures killed the doctor, escaped into the woods, and created a tunnel system where they supposedly live today. Some people swear they've seen glowing eyes watching them from the woods at night. Others say if you stop your car for too long, they'll crawl under it and ride home with you.

One thing everyone agrees on: they live in the woods around the mansion we'll be staying in. *Greeeeeeat.*

Leo's eyes widen. "What kind of mutant creatures? Like coyotes or something?"

I shake my head slowly at him, a feral smile on my lips. "Oh no. The creatures are worse, so much worse than coyotes."

"Stop," Dad says sternly. "Those rumors are not true. They're just silly campfire stories people around here tell to scare each other, that's all."

Maybe. "But if the mansion is awesome *and* the Hitchhiker stories are totally fake, then why did the museum people hire you?" I pose. Mom always says, "Where there's smoke, there's fire." And these creature rumors are the smoke. Question is, is there actually fire, or is Dad right and it's all made up?

"I already went over this with you, Ginny. Please don't fire up that imagination of yours and come up with a reason to panic, okay?" Dad answers.

I sink back into my seat, frustrated. Of course, he would blame me for the Hitchhiker stories. Mom and Dad think I ask too many questions and panic when there's no reason to. But

I just like to look at all the possibilities. I feel around in my pocket for the wild animal whistle I got at the camping store before we left. The internet told me there *are* bears here, and if one of them shows up, my family will be pretty grateful that I'm prepared!

"Hold up," Leo hops out of the car and tosses his basketball on the seat before shutting the door. "What the heck is a Hitchhiker?"

"It's a made-up thing, and we're done talking about it!" Dad snaps. He rubs his temples and sighs. "I'm sorry. I just don't want to start this trip off on the wrong foot. Can we all just agree not to pay any attention to these ridiculous stories?"

"I agree with your father. Let's try to look on the bright side. You two will be staying in a sixteen thousand-square-foot mansion. A mansion! You're going to feel like royalty." Mom pulls Leo in for an awkward hug. I step away. Maybe I'll eventually forgive them, but not yet.

Dad notices. He motions for Mom and Leo to walk on ahead. Refocusing on me, he makes a face that reminds me of the time I convinced Leo to eat a whole lemon. "Look. Your mother is giving up an entire month of tutoring to be here with us, and your brother probably could have found a basketball camp to attend. The two of them are making the best of it. If you tried, I think you'd find that not everything here is miserable."

Just as the words leave his lips, the sun comes out. A gentle breeze wafts the smell of lake water past my nose. I scan the area, noticing for the first time that the street we parked on is nice. Cute, actually. Flowers line the sidewalks and boutique shops advertise everything from homemade jam to hand-knit scarves.

"I guess it's not that bad. Is the mansion close?" I ask, trying to be positive even though my insides feel as black as Mom's charred cookies.

Dad fishes his cell phone out of his pocket and presses the home button. A map lights up the screen. "It's only about three miles away. Here's where we are now." He points to a little blue arrow. "And here's Woodmoor."

A long silence draws out between us. Dad stuffs his phone back in his pocket. "Did I mention you get to pick your room first?"

I perk up. "Before Leo?"

"Before any of us." A wide smile stretches across his face. "All I ask in return is that you go into this with an open mind. Just focus on enjoying the beautiful place we're staying in and having a good summer. Deal?"

I take another look around downtown Saugatuck. There's a *help wanted* sign hanging in the window of a bookstore across the street. Maybe they would hire a twelve-year-old. I'd be great at recommending mystery books to their customers. I'd even do boring work like shelve stuff if they'd let me. I glance back at Dad, feeling hopeful for the first time. "Deal."

CHAPTER THREE

Swatting Leo away from the last of my sub sandwich, I jam it into my mouth before climbing back into the car. Can't take any risks when you're around my brother. Mom jokes that he has a bottomless stomach, but I think it might actually be true.

The car rumbles to life as we head toward our home for the next month. Outside my window, the cute restaurants and shops vanish one by one. Soon I'm left staring at a stretch of deserted-looking road. Tall, spindly trees wind up toward the sky on each side, giving the street a dark, canopied feeling.

"The websites weren't kidding," I mumble.

Mom looks up from her phone and out at the trees in question. "About what, honey?"

"This place really is in the middle of nowhere." The road narrows until it becomes just two thin lanes weaving through more dense forest, the forest that the Hitchhikers supposedly live in.

"The mansion is on the edge of a state park. It will be quiet...peaceful," Dad says. "No noisy traffic or police sirens. Just us and the beauty of Michigan." Dad catches my skeptical expression from the rearview mirror. "I'm serious! The city is great but tiring. Consider this an opportunity to unwind and truly rest for once."

The next road we turn down is even more narrow than the last. It's two lanes and snakelike, winding through thick, towering trees. When the trees on the right side finally open to reveal a pasture and a mammoth brick building sitting in the middle of it, I gasp. That's it? That's Woodmoor?

It's... It's...

"Spooky," Leo says, reading my mind.

"Pffft," Dad answers with a snort. "Woodmoor Manor is amazing. If it looks spooky to you, that's only because it's on the outskirts of town. You're city kids! You're not used to staying in remote places."

"Plus, it's cloudy out. That makes everything look more somber," Mom adds in a chipper voice.

Nope. The mansion isn't spooky because it's remote, or because the clouds suddenly snuck in and swallowed the sun. It's spooky because it looks like a giant Halloween decoration.

My eyes sweep across the building as we draw closer. It's not just big; it's huge. At least thirty darkened windows are nestled into brown brick, and several aging columns flank the large doorway. Zero chance this place is anything but ugly inside. It's probably a wreck, and I'll end up sleeping on a cot or in a sleeping bag. Or maybe I'll get super unlucky and fall through some hidden weak spot in the floor.

We follow the winding road as it curves around the side of the mansion and ends at a parking lot. A cluster of people at the edge are taking pictures of the house. When they see us, they quickly lower their phones and start walking toward the only other car sitting in the lot.

"What were they doing? Why were they taking pictures of the house like that?" I ask.

"Probably just interested in the history," Dad replies. "Or the architecture."

I watch as their car slowly idles past, their wide eyes trained on Woodmoor. They don't look like history nerds. Or architecture nerds. They look...excited? Just before their car leaves the lot, I notice the bumper stickers plastered all over the back. One of them reads:

WARNING: THIS VEHICLE MAKES SUDDEN STOPS AT HAUNTED HOUSES.

So that explains it. The same kind of people that like

haunted houses probably also like Hitchhiker legends. They were probably here taking pictures of the place where the Hitchhikers roam around at night, looking for campers to snatch up. *The place I'm staying for the next month.*

Getting out of the car, I stare, unblinking at the sight in front of us. A field of green stretches out into the distance. It's surrounded by curtains of dark swaying trees.

Mom heaves my suitcase from the trunk and plops it on the cement in front of me with a thud. She gently jostles my shoulder. "Ginny?"

"Yeah. Sorry." I snag my suitcase absentmindedly, my gaze snapping back to the mansion. It's dark. Unsettling. The shadowy tree line lingers in the background like a warning. I narrow my eyes on a wooden sign dangling lopsidedly from a post. The words NO CAMPING are scrawled across it in white paint. An unseasonably cool breeze suddenly snatches my hair and whips it into my face. I fight off a shudder.

Summer wasn't supposed to be like this.

"You're right," Leo says in a hushed tone.

I turn toward my brother, startled by the grim expression on his face. "What?"

"This *is* bad."

CHAPTER FOUR

I drag my suitcase up the path toward the house. Scraggly flowers sit in chipped planters along the path, and a rickety old wooden bench is perched outside the front door. The grass in the front lawn looks half-dead. It's light green, almost yellow, with patches of brown here and there. My eyes flick back to the building, pausing briefly on a section of brick by the front door that looks like there's writing on it.

To...

The bushes shift in the wind, covering the rest of the words.

The heavy, wooden door of Woodmoor Manor swings open with a groan. Dad drags a few suitcases inside, then holds the door while we follow him in.

Squinting to adjust to the darkness, I get my first glimpse of the inside of our summer home. A hallway stretches out in front of us. Old-fashioned light fixtures hang on the faded yellow walls, a few random paintings perched in between them. At the end of the hall, a large square window allows just enough sunlight in for me to make out the stairwell leading upstairs.

Tick.

Tick.

Tick...

The distant sound of something ticking draws my attention from the steps. I squeeze my suitcase handle tighter, suddenly wishing we were anywhere but here.

"Well? What do you guys think?" Dad asks, shaking me from the trance I'm in.

I think it smells weird. Musty, like the clothes in Grandma Annie's old cedar chest. "It's nice," I say, gritting my teeth around the lie. Dad already feels bad and I don't want to make him feel worse. He's just clueless sometimes. Even though I'm annoyed with him, with *this*, I know he didn't bring us to Michigan to ruin our summer.

"It *is* nice, isn't it?" Mom chirps, grinning. "It's exactly what we need this summer. Fresh air, friendly people."

I smile weakly, wishing I could be more like Mom and

ignore the awful vibe this place has going on. She's one of the most positive people I know.

Still. I'm not sure how she can be quite so positive about the mansion we're standing in right now. Even if I were into old buildings—which I'm definitely not—this place would give me the chills.

Running a hand over the frame of a painting, Mom smiles wistfully. "They did a wonderful job of restoring the first time, but I do see why they want to work with you. It could be a little less...ahh, ominous?"

An impish grin breaks out on Dad's face, the one he wears when things are going his way. Funny how his way always seems to be the opposite of mine. We're like oil and water, Dad and me. He sees possibilities in this place. I see... well, old stuff mainly. Whatever. It's the things I *don't* see that bother me most, anyway. I don't see Erica, and I don't see my cozy bed, which I was planning to sleep late in every day. I don't even see a television!

"Agreed. The tone is a little somber in here," Dad says, peeking into the next room. "I just hope it isn't too late to change the perception of this place. It's so charming."

We leave our suitcases in the hallway and follow Dad on a tour of the main floor. There's a huge room with an old-fashioned couch and a fireplace in it, a dining room with walls completely covered by a mural of a castle and men riding horses, and a kitchen. It's the kitchen that catches my eye, mainly because it's so simple. Plain white cabinets adorn the walls. No fancy appliances. Even the stove is small; it only has four burners instead of six like our one at home.

There goes Mom's resolution.

"How are you going to bake here?" I ask. "Looks kinda small and empty."

Mom drops her hands to her hips and nods. "Oh, I don't know. I think it's just fine. I'm not a professional, so it's not like I need much."

"What about a mixer?" I think of the brand-new mixer Mom has at home. She just bought it a month ago and now it's her pride and joy. Maybe if she left it, we'd have to go back. And maybe if we had to go back, Dad would decide this whole idea is a waste of time and he'd change his mind. "You can't bake without a mixer."

Mom flashes me a knowing smile. "I'll be fine. The mixer is in the trunk of the car, and if I discover I've forgotten anything important, there's a wonderful cooking store in town."

My shoulders sag.

After seeing the library and another eating area, we circle back around to the front hall where our luggage is waiting. I squint at the light streaming in through the windows on either side of the front door, realizing for the first time how dark the rest of the house is. Like a tomb.

Nudging my shoulder, Dad's smile widens. "So? You gonna go?"

I blink at him, confused. "Go where?"

"Pick out your room! Remember?"

Oh. That. I glance back at the darkened stairwell, anxiety rolling around inside me like a summer storm. The bedrooms are probably all upstairs. They are in our house back in Chicago. Do I want to go upstairs? I swallow hard, trying to ignore the ticking sound that's beginning to suffocate me.

My brother sighs and takes a step toward the stairwell. Oh no he doesn't. I snag his T-shirt and tug him backward. "Not so fast. Dad said I have first pick."

"Fine," he grumbles. "But make it fast, okay? I'm starving."

I snort. When is my brother *not* starving?

"So, um, anywhere? Just go up and look around?" I ask, hoping Dad will offer to go up with me.

"You got it. There are eight bedrooms up there, so I'm sure you'll find one that suits you." He goes to grab some luggage but turns back abruptly. "Oh, I almost forgot. No touching the display items."

Leo's eyebrows knit together. "Isn't everything here a display item? It's all old, right?"

Dad waffles his hand in the air. "Yes and no. In some rooms there are displays meant to show a little about the life of the man who owned this home. There's some original clothing and personal items like vases and mirrors. They're labeled, so it shouldn't be hard to tell what's off-limits. I promised the head of the historical society that we'd be respectful, so no hands—okay?"

I nod. I don't want to touch the old clothes, anyway. I don't even really want to go upstairs right now, but no way am I gonna let Leo get first pick.

Dragging my suitcase behind me, I make my way up the stairwell. My luggage thumps against each step, sounding more like a warped heartbeat than wheels on wood. By the time I reach the top, I'm sweating. Literally. Tiny drops of sweat are beaded up at my hairline and my pits are swampy.

No air conditioning. *Awesome.*

A wooden bench rests at the top of the stairs, and a stained-glass window sits above it. I'd planned on just claiming the first room I came across, but as I step into it, I realize that's not gonna work. It's pink. *Really* pink. Pink walls, pink rugs, and pink bedding. It looks like a unicorn puked in here.

The second bedroom isn't much better. It's decorated in a delicate floral pattern, which isn't awful, but instead of one big bed there are two twin beds. I shake my head and laugh. The person who bought this furniture must not have been a big sleeper because everyone knows big beds are better for sleeping in than small ones.

Turning on my heel, I walk toward the opposite end of the hall where light is coming in from a doorway on the left. I follow it, my mood lifting when I find myself standing in the center of an enormous bedroom with an even more enormous bed.

Jackpot!

There's a fireplace on one wall and two windows on either side. A crystal chandelier hangs from the ceiling. I swallow back an unexpected jolt of excitement. I'm still not happy, but a fireplace *and* a chandelier? Nice! I turn a full circle, noticing there's another room connected by double doors. It's pretty empty except for a small desk and couch. It's also *all* windows—like a sunroom! Probably the reason this room feels so much brighter than anywhere else I've seen.

Brighter.

Yup. This is it. This is my room.

I'm just about to explore the bathroom situation when Leo's annoyed voice drifts up the stairs.

"You get lost, dork? C'mon!"

I roll my eyes even though he can't see me. "I'm done. Sheesh. Come on up. Plenty of choices left for you."

Stifling a laugh with my hand, I imagine my six-foot-tall

brother in the pink room or squished into one of the small beds. Even though he's not that much older than me, Leo is huge. I don't get it. He just keeps growing. Meanwhile, it seems like the growth fairy pushed the pause button on me.

Pulling my suitcase into the corner, I lean it against the wall and make my way back to the stairs. Unpacking can wait. Besides, I want to be around when Leo notices there's no...

"Hey! Where are the TVs in this place?"

The laughter I've been trying to hold in escapes. My brother abandons his suitcase in a room down the hall from mine, then crashes past me, his face scrunched up into a mess of confusion as he searches one room after the other.

"What kind of mansion doesn't have proper entertainment equipment?" he asks Dad, who is wrestling the rest of our luggage to the top of the steps.

"The original kind," Dad answers flatly. "This home was built in nineteen thirty-eight, Leo. Televisions had been invented but weren't common in households yet."

Leo eyes my parents warily. "So, there's none here? Not one?"

"It wouldn't be very authentic if there were, would it?" Dad poses.

Mom purses her lips together. It looks like she's trying not to smile. "You'll survive, Leo. Look at this as an opportunity to read a good book or take a walk. Explore the state park. I've heard it's amazing!"

My brother looks crestfallen. I don't blame him. He plays so many video games at home sometimes I wonder if he'd die without them. Guess we'll find out.

Leo wanders back into his chosen room, muttering something about a nightmare and how there'd better be actual bathrooms and not outhouses.

Dad pauses in the doorway of the room I've chosen. "This is your room, huh?"

There's a strange tone in his voice. I stop snooping around long enough to look at him. His eyebrows are pinched together, and his mouth has settled into something that's not quite a frown, but definitely not a smile, either. "Yeah. Is that okay?"

"Sure. Of course." He glances around and taps on the doorframe. "Alrighty, then. Guess I better go see if Mom has picked out our room yet."

I nod and follow him into the hall. That was weird. Maybe I accidentally took the room he wanted?

Mom apparently settled on a room in the middle of the hallway. I peek in, noting it's similar to mine, only smaller and doesn't have a sunroom. It's also on the opposite side of the house, so the view from their window is of the tree line. My eyes linger on the trees—the trees that stay dark even in broad daylight. A breeze sends them swaying, their movements synchronized and eerie. I watch the inky darkness stretched between the trunks, and for a second, I understand why everyone around here thinks the forest is scary. It doesn't just look dark or spooky.

It looks alive.

CHAPTER FIVE

One hour later and I'm standing over a half-unpacked suitcase, staring at the *thing* in the corner. The thing I didn't notice when I picked this room, probably because my troll of a brother was rushing me.

A mannequin. It's tucked into the corner and wearing some kind of old-fashioned gown. Black and blue sequins drip from every inch of it, creating a flickering pattern of light on the wall. My eyes skip from the dress to the head. It's covered in brown hair that's drawn into a bun and secured with sparkly barrettes. But the face, the face is...missing. There are no painted eyes. No strawberry-tinted cheeks. No mouth. There's nothing but skin-colored fabric stretched tight over a bump that's probably supposed to be a nose.

Crouching down in front of it, I scour the dress for the display label Dad talked about. It's not there. I lean back on my heels, my brain racing. I can totally imagine waking up at night and mistaking this mannequin for a bedazzled burglar. Nope, nope, nope.

I snag an old quilt from the back of the couch, laughing bitterly at my crummy luck. Leo probably has a pretty vase in his room, but I get *this*. A faceless mannequin. I toss the quilt over it and cringe as it precariously rocks side to side on its rickety pedestal. Once it finally balances itself again, I let out the breath I was holding.

Ginnnnnny.

A raspy whisper startles me. Spinning around, I brace myself for Leo to pop out from behind something. I don't know how he did it, since my brother has never been quiet in his entire life, but he must've managed to sneak in while I was examining the mannequin. My anger builds as I imagine him tucked behind a piece of furniture, trying not to laugh. Jerk.

"The whole *stay out of my room* thing doesn't change just because we aren't in Chicago anymore, Leo," I growl out.

Silence.

Fine. Two can play at his game. I drop down onto all fours and look under the bed. It's crammed full of storage containers. Definitely nowhere for him to hide there. Pulling upright, I turn a full circle. Seriously. How is my Sasquatch of a brother hiding in this room? Other than the bed, there's no furniture big enough to cover him completely.

I fling open the door of the connected bathroom and jump inside. The shower has a glass door instead of a curtain, so I can see it's empty. Walking back out into my room, I stand still and listen. The only sound is the slightly softer but still present tick, tick, ticking of that stupid clock. He's here, though. No way he left before getting the chance to really terrify me.

"Why are you doing this?" I plead, even though I know the answer. If there's one thing older brothers like to do, it's tease. I hate it.

"Come out, Leo. I'm not joking anymore." I can feel the waves of panic beginning to crash over me. My cheeks heat up with embarrassment. I will not get scared of stupid sounds. I will not get scared of stupid sounds. I will not...

Ginnnny.

This time I shriek. *Stay calm, Ginny. This is exactly what he wants. He's probably taking a video right now so he can make you look like an idiot on Snapchat.*

Inhaling deeply, I tell myself to be brave. No screaming, no matter how much I want to. Instead, I focus on searching the corners and behind the bathroom door. Empty, empty, empty. Crossing the room, I lift a shaking hand to sweep aside the heavy curtains on either side of the biggest window. A few stray dust bunnies tumble out, but no Leo.

I'm just about to jab the pointy end of an umbrella I found up into the fireplace when Dad walks in.

"Ginny?" His expression is bewildered. "What on earth are you doing?"

Rushing over, he takes the umbrella and turns it over in his hands, then holds it out to reveal a small rectangular label.

1828

Oops. Guess I found another display item.

I drop my head into my hands. "I'm sorry! I didn't know. Leo is in here trying to scare me, and"—I glance back at the fireplace, which I now realize is *way* too small for my brother to have climbed up—"I thought he might be up there."

Dad arches an eyebrow. "What do you mean Leo is in here?"

"He's hiding somewhere," I grind out, waving my hands in the air. "Keeps whispering my name to freak me out."

"That's not possible, honey," he responds quietly. "I'm not sure what you heard, but I know it wasn't Leo."

"Why? I heard him clearly. Twice!"

He shakes his head, his mouth downturned into a slight frown. "Because he's in the kitchen with your mother."

CHAPTER SIX

It's not possible. I heard Leo say my name twice. I replay the sound in my head. It was my name for sure, but is it possible it wasn't Leo? The idea sends a jolt of fear through me.

"You're positive Leo's in the kitchen?"

Dad nods. "I just left him there with Mom. They were unloading some kitchen supplies."

"Okay. Maybe he beat you up the stairs? He is pretty fast," I say.

"Ahh, I don't think so. I walked directly from the kitchen up here to check on you. Leo would've had to hurdle me to get up here first." Dad takes in the scowl on my face and his own frown deepens. "Are you sure it wasn't just the wind, kiddo? Mom just heard on the radio we're supposed to get a whopper of a storm tonight."

"No!" I snap, then shake my head. "I mean, it wasn't the wind. It was my name and it was coming from somewhere in this room!"

Just then a cackle echoes through the room—*a Leo cackle*. Dad's eyes widen for a moment, then narrow on a small glint of silver on the wall by the bed.

"The speaking tube," he says with a labored sigh. "Leo found the speaking tube."

"The what?" I ask, taking a few steps closer to the silver knob Dad is staring at. No, not a knob. A pipe.

Dad presses his mouth closer to the pipe stuck in the wall. "Not cool, Leonardo. Not cool at all. Your sister was terrified!"

"Sorry," my brother's sheepish voice echoes from the pipe. "Just thought it would be funny."

I gasp. "What is that? Why can Leo talk into my bedroom like that?"

"When this house was built, speaking tubes were the newest technology. Wealthier people with large homes would have them installed so that the maids could communicate when they were on different floors."

Eyeing the tube, I try to imagine how the contraption works. "So, it's a tube that connects different rooms? They'd just talk into it?"

"Pretty much! There are three in this house. This one,

one in the kitchen, and one in the hallway outside of what used to be the maids' quarters."

"So, Leo found the one in the kitchen and decided to torment me with it. What a brother."

Dad drops a hand to my shoulder and gives it a squeeze. "It wasn't nice of him, honey, but he didn't anticipate scaring you for real. Leo is...*Leo*, but he's not mean."

No, he's not mean. He's just obnoxious and careless and completely annoying. I can't believe we didn't murder each other on the car ride here! I also can't believe I'm stuck in this house with him for a whole month. At least back home he'd have his friends and basketball to distract him. Here? Plenty of time to bug me.

"Look, I'm going to go downstairs and have a talk with him right now about that speaking tube." He says *talk* like he's going to punish Leo, which makes me feel slightly better. But Leo always manages to get himself out of trouble. "He won't be using it again, okay?"

I nod like I'm fine, but tears are still stinging at the edges of my eyelids. I blink several times, warning them not to fall. I'm not a baby and crying right now would be giving Leo the win.

"You swear Leo won't use that tube again?"

Dad shoots me a promising smile. "He won't if he ever wants to see a basketball court again."

That's good enough for me. I give a little wave as Dad leaves, then start picking up my overturned suitcase. My room might have a creepy spy-tube in it, but it's still the best one in the house, and I'm at least going to try to enjoy it.

CHAPTER SEVEN

It took forever, but I'm finally unpacked. Spreading my arms out into a t-shape, I fall forward, landing face-first on the bed. An *oof* sound whooshes out of me. Funny. That's how I feel right about now...*oof*. We just got here, and I already miss home. Chicago. My room. Erica. This will be the first time I can remember that we haven't seen each other for a whole month.

Rolling over, I snatch my phone off the nightstand and type out a quick text. Miss you. Two red words pop up just beneath my message. Not delivered.

What? Why?

I try again and get the exact same message. Jumping up, I walk toward the door to see if my signal is better in the hall. I have to be able to talk to Erica. Being stuck here is bad enough; I don't want to be completely cut off from my best friend too.

A rustle at my window catches my attention. I turn around to look, realizing that at some point, it got dark outside. Beyond my window I can barely see the outline of the trees— nothing but tall swaying shadows. Another sound breaks the silence. This time it's not a rustle. It's a squeal, like nails dragging across a chalkboard.

Warning bells go off in my brain. This is probably how all the stories about the Hitchhikers start. An innocent person hears a noise and before they know it, they're being slurped down like a Popsicle on a hot day by some awful creature. Laughing nervously, I tell myself the legends are just that. *Legends*. Campfire stories, like Dad said. There's nothing lurking outside. Nothing but...

My eyes freeze on the window. Long, bony fingers appear at the bottom, then begin inching their way up the glass. They tap, tap, tap against it, then slowly drag back down. The squeal echoes through the room again, making the hair on the back of my neck stand up.

Backing up, I fumble for the doorknob. My eyes stay glued to the fingers, still creeping upward as if they're headed for the lock. Just then, the hand pulls back and smacks the glass.

The doorknob begins turning in my palm. No! I grip it tighter and plant my foot against the door to keep it shut.

I don't know what's happening, but I do know that I didn't survive the three-hour drive here with Leo just to be killed on my first night.

Something bangs on my door now, the knob rattling frantically in my hand. I immediately think of the Hitchhikers—their glowing eyes and big heads. Maybe the people in this town aren't wrong. Maybe the Hitchhikers are crawling out of the woods this very moment and trying to get into my room! I press my whole body into the door to hold it shut, sweat beading on my forehead.

"Ginny? Is everything okay? Your door is stuck."

It's Mom. I let out the breath I was holding and move my foot.

Nudging my door open, Mom steps in. She's holding a bouquet of different spatulas and has four aprons hanging from her neck. The top one reads: *Life is short, lick the bowl.*

She looks me up and down. "What's going on?"

I swivel my head to look back at the window. The fingers are gone, replaced with the gnarled limb of a tree. It grazes the glass with a gust of wind, making the scraping sound again.

"Um, yeah. Sorry about that. I thought I saw something."

"Like what?" Mom asks.

"A creepy hand?" I shrug, then laugh weakly. "It was scratching at the window."

Just saying it out loud scares me all over again. Meanwhile, Mom bursts into laughter. "A creepy hand? Goodness, Ginny. We need to get you reading some other books. All those mystery novels have really gone to your head."

I wish her reaction surprised me, but it doesn't. Mom and Dad tell me all the time they wish my imagination were just a little less active. They'll never let me forget that a month ago I interrupted one of Mom's tutoring sessions because I thought our neighbor Mr. Goodie was burying a body in his backyard. Mom eventually gave in and marched over to his house to investigate. Turns out he was just planting tomatoes. In my defense, though, Mr. Goodie *is* strange. I mean, who wears Crocs year-round anyway?

I bite down on the inside of my cheek, feeling the familiar sting of embarrassment. I shouldn't have said anything.

"So, what's with all the aprons?" I ask, hoping to change the subject.

Mom looks down as if she forgot about them. "Oh! Yes. I was unpacking my luggage, and I remembered that I'd packed these aprons in my suitcase rather than the kitchen utensils box. I have so many other things to carry downstairs, I thought wearing them might free up my hands a bit."

She twirls around like she's modeling, the mess of aprons and apron strings whipping out around her like a tornado.

I giggle. "Well no matter what anyone says, it's a good look. I think all chefs should wear four aprons."

"Well I don't know about being a chef. I'm pretty far from that right now, don't you think?" She nudges me with her elbow, grinning.

"The cookies *were* a little hard."

"Like rocks," Mom adds with a laugh. "Don't worry! Next batch will be perfect! Or at least edible." She tucks a stray piece of auburn hair back up into her ponytail and waggles her eyebrows. "Hey, I have an idea. Since we don't really have groceries here yet, why don't we head back into town and grab dinner. You in?"

I shrug. "Sure."

"Have you looked around anymore?" she continues. "With twenty-six rooms in this house, there's a lot to explore!"

I'd forgotten there are so many rooms. I'll have to learn my way around fast, or I might get lost. "Why did they make this house so big, anyway? Wasn't it just for two people?"

"I think the man who built it wanted it to be a summer home big enough for their grown children and grandchildren to come visit. According to your father, family was very important to the owners."

Mom snakes an arm around my shoulders and reels me in for a hug. It makes me warm on the inside.

"I know this trip is hard on you, but your father... He appreciates it." With a gentle smile, she ruffles my hair just like she used to when I was small. Her eyes are apologetic.

"I know," I mumble.

"You're a lot like your father, kiddo. He's very passionate about his job, as passionate as you are about writing. Maybe spending a month in a new place will be interesting. Maybe you'll even come up with some new story ideas."

Her eyes twinkle with hope as she waits for my response. When it doesn't come, she reaches out and pats my hand. "Look, even if you go back to Chicago saying you never want to see Saugatuck again, your father will be grateful you helped him. He needs you."

"I'll try to like it." I shoot her a weak smile. "Promise."

She squeezes my hand gently. "Thank you. It's one month, honey. Just one. I'm excited about the opportunity to switch gears for a bit, you know?"

I do know. Mom is swamped back in Chicago. Between her regular tutoring kids and her always-panicked ACT and SAT prep kids, she never has time to relax. I guess she'll be able to do that here. Come to think of it, this might be the first real vacation I've ever seen Mom take.

I hold my phone up in the air and give it a shake. "Hey, I tried to text Erica, but my phone isn't working very well. Is yours?"

Mom takes it from my hand and examines the screen. "I haven't really tried to use mine, but you only have one bar. Oops, no bars. No, one. It keeps changing."

"So, does that mean there's no reception here or something?"

"Unfortunately, it's looking likely. Dad has made a couple calls since we got here, so there must be some areas of the house that get a decent signal, but your room sure isn't one of them."

I take my phone back and toss it on the bed. That's a hassle. How am I going to stay in touch with Erica like this?

"Dinner time?" she asks hopefully. "I heard a rumor that there's an amazing bakery in town too. Perhaps our first night here calls for a little dessert."

I glance back at the window one last time. The branch tapping against it is still just a branch. Breathing out a sigh of relief, I follow her out of the room.

CHAPTER EIGHT

Wow. Dad says that about one thousand people live in Saugatuck year-round. Tonight it seems like all one thousand of them are trying to eat dinner in the same restaurant.

Mom fights her way back through the crowd from the hostess desk. Her normally carefree face is pinched. "The wait is about forty-five minutes. Sorry. Guess this is a really popular tourist destination in the summer."

I look at the people already sitting in booths and jealousy needles me. Not only are they eating pizza that's making my mouth water, but they're probably staying in some awesome hotel on the beach. Unlike us, they just spent the day relaxing by the pool. They walked here because their place is so close to all the cute shops and restaurants. I think about the disturbing forest we have to drive past to get here and frown.

"I've got good news!" Dad's face suddenly appears in front of mine.

I must look confused because he chuckles. "Just found out they can seat us in the back if we're only going to get the buffet. It won't have as many choices as the main menu, but it will get us eating much faster. Is that okay with you?"

"Yes! I'm starving." I snap out of my funk and follow my family to the rear of the restaurant where a smaller room is crowded with families. Strollers line the back wall, mothers balance trays and toddlers, and one very frantic-looking waitress is ducking and weaving through it all. I dodge a napkin sailing through the air, exploding into laughter as it slaps against the side of Leo's head. He peels it off, grimacing.

"Bet you're glad you don't know what was on that," I tease.

"Shut up," he fires back, swiping at the side of his face with a sleeve.

"Probably some chewed-up pizza, some spit, and about eighty gazillion germs," I count off on my fingers, still feeling salty about his speaking tube prank. Leo doesn't like people to know, but he has a weak stomach. Once he threw up because he found a hair in his spaghetti.

Leo's face reddens. "I said *shut up*, Ginny!"

The room goes quiet. A few children snicker and at least

a half-dozen parents shoot a disgusted look in my brother's direction.

Dad turns to face us, an admonishing expression on his face. "Enough, you two! I know things didn't start off very well, but it's over. I don't want to hear another word out of either of you!"

I mumble an agreement and pull my chair out to sit. Leo stealthily hooks his foot around a leg and tries to pull it out from under me. I grip the back of it tighter, shaking my head as if to say *nice try, buddy.*

Yanking the chair back toward me, I plaster a smile on my face. Leo will not get to me, no matter how hard he tries. I've lived with him long enough to know all his tricks. I also know eventually he'll lose his cool and do something really dumb. He's already on strike one with Mom and Dad; a couple more, and he might end up grounded the whole time we're here. I linger on that thought. Now *that* would make up for what he did back at the mansion!

The waitress brings a pile of plates to the table. Leo takes off before any of us. I watch him hurdle a baby car seat, wondering if there will be anything left on the buffet by the time I get up there.

I'm heaping an epic pile of mashed potatoes on my plate when something bumps me from behind. A boy. He looks up from his own plate and smiles. "Sorry. It's a little crowded in here."

"A little? I'm pretty sure this is a major fire hazard." Just then a girl in pigtails runs by, accidentally stomping on my toe. I jump up and down on one foot, groaning. "Yup. Definitely a fire hazard."

He laughs and rakes a hand through his hair. It's light brown with gold highlights like he's been in the sun a lot. "Totally! I'm Will, by the way. You here for vacation?"

"Sorta. My dad has some research to do here, so he brought us along. I'm Ginny."

"Oh! Is he researching the dunes? I see people out there all the time taking samples of stuff."

A bitter laugh bubbles free. "Nope. He's researching the local architecture because he fixes up old buildings."

His face lights up. "Sweet! My dad's an accountant. Not a lot of cool research trips with that job."

I laugh along with him, my mind a million miles away from the dim lights, creaky floors, and random ticking in the mansion.

"So where are you staying?"

Dum, dum, duuuuuuum. I scrape my brain for an answer other than the truth but come up empty. I don't know the names of any hotels here! If Will visits Saugatuck every summer, he'll know I'm lying for sure if I try to make one up.

"Um, we're staying at the mansion just outside of town."

Will tilts his head to the side, studying me. "Do you mean the old Woodmoor place?"

I nod.

His smile vanishes.

"I didn't know you could stay there," he answers carefully. "I mean, I get that your dad is into architecture and stuff, but..." He lowers his voice. "You know what they say about that place, right?"

"You mean the *Hitchhikers*?" I joke, trying for a light-hearted laugh. Only it doesn't come out lighthearted. It's strained and fake.

Will looks to a table where a man is waving at him, then back to me. "The Hitchhiker stories, yeah. I mean, some people around here totally believe in them. But that's not the only legend around here."

"Okay, if you're trying to freak me out, it isn't working." I say this with a smile, so he knows I'm just joking.

"I'm not trying to scare you. Swear. Just...just be careful."

His tone isn't playful anymore. It's warning.

"Be careful? Of what? I don't—" I start.

Will holds a hand up to stop me. "Listen. Weird things have happened in that house for years. Unexplainable things. Everyone around here knows to stay away."

I'm about to ask what kind of unexplainable things he's talking about when a man's voice rises about the chatter.

"Will!" The waving man—probably his dad—is headed our way now. He doesn't look happy.

Will lets out a long sigh. "I gotta get back to my table. My dad is crazy about staying on a schedule when we're on vacation. It's so annoying, especially since we stay here every summer. It's like our second home."

Not as annoying as having a dad who drags you to a cursed mansion for vacation, but whatever.

"Don't worry about what I said. You'll be fine!" He tries to sound convincing but fails. "Just stay away from the ballroom."

Wait, what? There's a ballroom in the mansion?

"Thanks," I finally manage to spit out, cursing the heat in my cheeks. Will walks away with a small wave, leaving me at the buffet with a plate of cold potatoes and a *very* bad feeling.

CHAPTER NINE

"You sure you're okay, honey? You barely ate anything at dinner." Mom twists around in her seat to face me.

I look down at my lap. My ears are still ringing with what Will said.

"I'm fine. Just got a little carsick on the way there is all."

Leo lifts his head to look at me. The light from his cell phone brightens his face. His expression is odd. Unreadable.

"I think I'm just going to go to bed when we get back to the house if that's okay," I add, hoping everyone gets the hint and leaves me alone.

"Don't blame you a bit. It has been a long day." Dad turns onto the winding road that leads straight back to the mansion. He leans toward the windshield and flicks on the brighter headlights. They cut through the darkness, bathing the trees in an eerie glow. "If you don't mind, I just need a few minutes of your time before you hit the hay. You and Leo."

I sit up straighter. What could he possibly need us for?

As if he read my mind, Dad looks in the rearview mirror and laughs. "Relax, guys. It's not a big deal. Ten minutes tops. We need to carry some boxes of utensils up into storage so the kitchen will be a little more open for Mom to work."

"Upstairs? You mean, like into one of the extra bedrooms?" Leo asks.

"No. Into the ballroom on the third floor."

My heart gallops around in my chest at the idea of going into the one room that Will guy told me to avoid.

I tell myself to get a grip. This is stupid. For all I know, he was just trying to scare me. Maybe Will isn't nice at all. Maybe he actually lives here year-round and his hobby is terrorizing tourists! *Still.* It didn't seem that way. He seemed nice. Honest. And if he was acting, then he should move to Hollywood because he's good.

"Couldn't we just stick the boxes into one of the extra bedrooms?" I ask.

Dad appears to think about it, then shakes his head. "The ballroom has the most space. It's also out of the way. Probably best to put everything up there for now."

I try to hold in my groan. It comes out anyway, sounding more like a whimper.

Dad pulls the car into a parking spot and turns it off, then pats my mom on the leg. "Your mother is going to finish putting new sheets on all the beds, so I told her we'd handle this."

"No problem," I say, lifting my chin defiantly. I won't let these legends ruin my summer any more than I'll let Leo ruin it. "I can help."

Leo rolls his eyes at me. I roll mine back. Sometimes I swear he spends most of his time trying to get on my nerves.

I lean against the car, pretending to scrape something off the bottom of my shoe while the rest of my family heads toward the house. As soon as they walk through the front door, I bend down and peer underneath the car. It's empty. No glowing eyes or gnarled fingers. No Hitchhikers. Standing back up, I glance at my bedroom window. There's a soft glow coming from inside, probably the bathroom light I left on. The tree I saw earlier is gently rocking back and forth.

I'm about ready to go inside when I hear it. The *crunching*. It's coming from the woods and sounds like someone walking through leaves in October, only it isn't October, and there shouldn't be anyone else out here.

I stiffen and squint into the shadows. "Hello?"

The crunching stops. I should just go inside. It's probably

nothing. Then again, the look on Will's face wasn't nothing. I feel around in my pocket for the animal whistle. It's not there. I must've left it in the house.

The snap of a twig echoes out from the same spot in the trees. I take a step forward, my heart rate quickening. Another step. Before I know it, I'm at the edge of the timber. The sounds of summer slowly fade into nothingness as I stare into the dark. I can just barely make out the NO CAMPING sign, now swinging side-to-side in the breeze. The high-pitched squeak of its edges rubbing against the post gives me goose bumps.

I'm just about to walk away when I hear the crunching again. It's closer than before. Too close. I take a step back, but it's too late. The bushes begin shaking, and a horrible, gut-wrenching squall pierces the silence. A dark shadow bursts out of the woods and runs directly at me. I stumble over a cement parking block and fall. Pain shoots up my thigh. Out of instinct I shield my face, hoping that whatever hideous forest monster I've awakened will eat something other than that. I *did* just get my braces off.

The shadow doesn't pounce and kill me, though. Instead, it runs past. Past me, past the car, past the house. It vanishes into the field in a streak of black and gray. *A raccoon.* I just about peed my pants over a raccoon. Seriously?

Standing up, I press a hand to my chest and focus on

breathing. This is what I get for letting strange boys freak me out with their stories!

"Ginny? Everything okay?" Dad calls out. He's holding the front door open, one eyebrow raised as if he's trying to figure out what I'm doing.

That makes two of us.

"Yeah. Everything is fine. I was just looking for something." I hustle toward the door, hating the darkness more and more with each step. Back in Chicago, it's never dark. In fact, I can't remember the last time it was dark enough outside for me to see a star in the sky. Here the only light is coming from the two itty-bitty porch lights on either side of the front door.

As soon as I step over the threshold, I hear the ticking again. I have to remember to look for that clock soon. If I find it, I'm gonna smash it with a hammer—display label or not!

We shrug off our coats, then hang them in the closet. Dad leads us back through the labyrinth of dim hallways to the kitchen, where an army of cardboard boxes is waiting for us.

Leo's mouth flops open. "We have to carry *all* these up to the third floor? There isn't an elevator or something we can use?"

Dad looks unimpressed. "Leo, if there are no televisions in this home, do you really think there is going to be an *elevator*?"

"Well, I don't know! Just seems bananas that they'd make such a big house with so many floors without thinking about... you know, folks with disabilities and stuff."

"Or lazy teenage boys," I say.

My brother levels an icy glare in my direction.

Dad points at a box labeled MISCELLANEOUS KITCHEN and tells Leo to grab it. Meanwhile, I pick up two huge canvas bags filled with supplies and hoist one over each of my shoulders. We follow Dad upstairs, down the hall past our bedrooms, and to the end where there's another set of steps. A very narrow set.

I pause at the bottom and adjust the bag straps that are digging painfully into my shoulders. Sweat trickles down my back. "You sure this doesn't go to an attic or something? These don't look like the type of stairs that would lead up to a ballroom."

Dad grunts a yes and starts trudging up. "That's part of my job here, guys. To figure out how to make this mansion more event-friendly. There are a lot of spaces that aren't ideal, but I need to figure out how to make them work without losing the historical integrity of—"

I immediately tune him out. I'm glad he likes his job and all but listening to Dad talk about it can be boring.

When we reach the top, it's dark. Dad walks ahead of us. I can hear him shuffling around but can't tell where he is. I stay frozen, wishing I'd kept up the whole carsickness story to avoid this. A creak from somewhere breaks the silence, followed by a thump and a clear "ouch."

"Dad?"

The lights flip on. I shield my eyes against the sudden brightness. When I finally look up, I see a room about the same size as our gym at school. It's got hardwood floors and is empty, except for a few tables and chairs shoved into the far corner. Large rectangular windows are set into the angled ceiling. Like the rest of the house, it's too dark. An unsettling feeling creeps over me, like I'm being watched. I cross my arms over my chest and try to shake it off. There's nothing in here.

"So, this ballroom. It's...interesting." I choose my words carefully. If I say too much, Dad will know I'm fishing for information, and he'll get suspicious.

Swiping the sweat from his forehead, Dad nods. "Sure is. Apparently, the wife liked the idea of entertaining friends and family."

"It's hot up here," Leo grumbles.

Rolling his eyes, Dad gestures toward the stairs. "You two mind getting the next boxes? I just realized your mother said *not* to stack these up. There's some fragile equipment in them. I'll get them resituated and see you two in a minute."

Leo stalks away immediately.

By the time I reach the kitchen, Leo has already left with his box. Mom isn't there, either. I'm just bending down to wrestle with a Tupperware bin full of baking tins when I hear the ticking again. It's louder than it has ever been, and it seems to be coming from...the speaking tube?

Creeping over, I slowly press an ear to the pipe. Sure enough, the ticking echoes out. Melodically. Hauntingly.

Alarms go off in my brain. According to Dad, this tube is connected to only two other places in the house. The hallway outside of the maids' quarters and *my room*. I pull my ear away from the pipe, a nervous energy rushing through me. I spent hours in my room this afternoon and never heard the ticking, not loudly anyway. It was always an echo, faint as if it was coming from somewhere farther away in the house.

Mom walks in, stopping short when she sees me. "Honey? You okay?"

I jerk away from the tube. "I think so. Um... Do you know where the maids' quarters are?"

A puzzled look crosses her face. "I can't say I've come across them yet. I think your father mentioned them being in the north end of the house."

"Down here?"

"No. Upstairs. I think there's an entire wing that used to

be dedicated to the servants." She laughs quietly. "Can you imagine having servants?"

I give her a tight smile. Truth is, I *can't* imagine having servants. A ton of my friends have a cleaning service that comes into their house once a week, but not us. My parents believe in doing that kind of stuff ourselves. That means no cleaning service for our cluttered house. No leaf-raking crew in the fall. No team of bundled-up people pushing snow blowers in the winter. Nothing but the four of us.

"No. Guess not. I better get this box to the ballroom."

Her eyes skim over the box in my hands. She unfolds the top flap, then shakes her head. "Oh! No need. There's room for these things in the drawers, so leave it here."

"Does that mean you guys don't need me anymore?" *Please say yes.*

"I'm sure Dad and Leo can handle the rest. I know you're tired and not feeling fantastic, so why don't you just hit the hay. Tomorrow is going to be a big day!"

I eye her warily. "Why? Do we have plans?"

"You mean other than getting settled in and exploring the house and town? And don't forget about all the gardens and trails you can roam around."

Gardens and trails that just *might* have Hitchhikers prowling in them. I mean, the legend had to come from somewhere, right? Even if only one person vanished in these woods, that's one too many!

"Plus," Mom continues, "I *might* have seen you chitchatting with a boy at dinner. Who knows? Maybe you'll run into him again." She tucks her folded aprons in a drawer, then winks in my direction.

Oh no. Mom is not going to convince me to talk about my conversation with Will. I'd rather stick a fork in my eyeball. Besides, she wouldn't like what we discussed.

"Right. I'll find something to do." I leave it at that. Tomorrow's plans can wait. Right now, I need to find the maids' quarters and Kill. That. Clock.

CHAPTER TEN

The maids' quarters aren't much different from the rest of the house. I trail my fingertips along the aging wallpaper as I walk down the dimly lit hall, wondering who stayed in these rooms all those years ago. It definitely wasn't a bad place to live, but cleaning this rambling old place day after day probably got pretty old.

And spooky.

The creaky floor is making it hard for me to listen for the clock, so I stop moving. Within seconds I hear it...the ticking. I frown. If the clock is hanging in this hall, the ticking should be louder. Instead, it's faint again, like the sound is echoing from a room on the other side of the house. How is that possible? I pop my head into each bedroom. The ticking is the same in all of them. Muffled, but present. Like a mosquito in the summer that won't stay away from your ear.

Running my hands down my face, I slide down the wall until my butt meets the floor. If there really are only three speaking tubes in the mansion, and the ticking isn't coming from this one, then I have a problem.

"What are you doing here?" Leo appears in the hallway. His forehead is speckled with sweat.

I scramble up off the floor. "Nothing. Just looking around is all."

The weird expression is back. The one from the car. Leo looks up and down the hallway, then narrows his eyes on me. "You've never been carsick."

"What?"

"In the car. You said you didn't eat dinner because you were feeling carsick, but I know that's not true. You ran up to the buffet like Ricky used to go after bones."

Ricky was our Labrador retriever. He died a year ago, but that dog *did* love his bones.

"And then I saw you talking to that guy," Leo continues. "Did he say something mean about your hair or your zit or something?"

"Ugh. No, Leo." I instinctively try to smooth down the wavier bits of my hair, wishing it didn't get so frizzy in the heat. And what zit? I feel around my chin until a familiar jolt of pain answers my question.

Oh.

Leo folds his arms over his chest and leans against the wall. "Then what's up? Why are you lying to Mom and Dad?"

"Why do you care?" Maybe the question is mean, but I never know what I'm getting with Leo. He *could* care about how I'm feeling, or he could be digging for information to hold over my head.

"I care because you've been acting wacky since we got here." He rolls his shoulders like he doesn't really care, but I know better. "It's throwing me off my game."

"Your game?" I repeat, snorting. My brother has such a big head sometimes. "Whatever. And I have *not* been acting wacky."

"Right. So, talking to strangers is normal for you?" He poses. "You're from Chicago, Ginny. We don't talk to people we don't know!"

"It's not like he was a wart-covered old woman offering me an apple," I snap. "Jeez. He was our age! Not exactly dangerous."

He smirks. I hate that smirk.

"Fair enough. What about all the other stuff, then? The car sickness that you've never had before. The freak-out in your room over a little whisper. The fact that you're sitting here in an empty hallway all by yourself. It's...weird!"

"The whisper freak-out was your fault!" I hiss back. If I had some, I'd dump fire ants in his bed. Or shave off one of his eyebrows while he sleeps. "And the other stuff is not a big deal. I'm fine. I came up here because I wanted to find the clock. The ticking is making me crazy."

I pause and listen again, scowling when ticking becomes clear again. "Can you hear it in your room?"

My brother cocks his head to the side. "Clock? What are you talking about?"

"The ticking!" I repeat and hold a finger up in the air, hoping he'll take the hint and listen. "Hear that? It's so annoying, and I can't find it to turn it off!"

"I don't hear anything, Gin," Leo says quietly.

My jaw drops. "What do you mean? It's so clear! Tick, tick, tick! It's like the thing is in every room at once! You don't hear that?"

He shakes his head, a grim expression settling on his face. "You hear it right now?"

I don't answer that. I don't need to. Leo's puzzled expression changes to a worried one in a flash.

"I should go to bed." I start to walk away, but he snags my elbow and pulls me back.

"Hey, don't let the rumors about this place get to you. This is just a dumb old house. Okay?"

"I know," I tell him with a sigh. It's embarrassing that he thinks he needs to say this. "I think I'm just tired. Tomorrow will be better."

"Okay." Leo lets go of my arm, but there's still a note of concern in his voice.

I shuffle down the hall back toward my room, lost in a fog of worry. By the time I reach the door, I'm convinced I must've imagined the clock. That would explain why no one else noticed it. Maybe the sound I heard was water dripping in the pipes. Dad always says old buildings have old pipes and the sounds they make can be scary sometimes. But if that's the case, then why didn't Leo hear it too?

Flinging open my door, my heart skips a beat. The ticking *is* here. It's no louder than it was in the maids' hallway, but it's clear.

I try to open the cabinet in the bathroom first. When the door doesn't budge, I press an ear to it and listen hard. The sound definitely isn't in there. I move on to the drawers under the sink and in the dresser. Other than a few lint balls and some extra toilet paper, they're empty. Definitely no clock. That's when I remember the storage containers under the bed. Maybe someone stowed the clock in there thinking the battery was dead, but it wasn't?

Getting down so I'm at eye level with the containers

again, I begin pulling them out. The first one is filled with old quilts. Second one contains a jumble of items: an old-fashioned looking hairbrush, a few hairpins, a wrap of some kind, and a beat-up old pair of heeled shoes.

The last box is the most curious. It contains another box—this one made of metal and held shut with an ornate silver lock. I hold the box up to my ear. It's silent. The ticking remains constant, but it's clearly not coming from any of the boxes beneath the bed.

Why can't Leo hear it? The thought needles me. Is it possible I have special hearing? I mean, I have heard of certain frequencies that kids can hear and adults can't. But this isn't a high-pitched sound, it's a low, melodic ticking. Like a countdown. A chill washes over me. I tell myself Leo could hear it if he really tried. If he sat down and stopped fidgeting and being loud, he'd hear it.

Right?

I shove all the containers back under my bed and decide to skip washing my face and brushing my teeth. Leo never brushes his and, so far, none have fallen out, so I don't think one night will kill me. I grab my headphones from the top of the dressing table and slide them on my head. A blissful quiet takes over as I peel back the covers and crawl into bed.

CHAPTER ELEVEN

A clap of thunder breaks through my headphones. Lurching awake, I glance at the window just in time to see a bolt of lightning shoot down toward the earth. Apparently, the storm has arrived. I sit upright and stare at the rain-streaked glass. The room that was once bright and sunny is now dark. Scary. Another flash of lightening brightens up the room and...

The mannequin. The blanket I tossed over it earlier in the day is now pooled on the floor. Its creepy faceless head is turned toward me. Was it facing my bed before? I can't remember. I squint through the darkness, wishing I'd chosen the room Leo is in.

Tugging the blankets up to my chin, I try to pretend I'm back home. I have the most beautiful room. Pale blue with stencils of birds that look like they're flying through my window. They're probably babyish. I mean, Mom did stencil them on when I was like six, but I love them. They're cheerful.

This place? Totally *not* cheerful. I thought I hit the jackpot with this room, but once the sun went down everything changed. Even the small bit of moonlight shining through the window isn't enough to make it feel friendly now.

A muffled knock jerks me from my thoughts. "Hello?"

I listen for Mom's or Dad's voice but hear nothing. Looking down at the gap beneath the door, I focus my eyes on the darkness. Just then, the hallway light flips on. Staring at the gap, I search for the shadow of Mom's fuzzy slippers. It isn't there. The hair on the back of my neck rises slowly. Something is wrong.

"Mom?" My voice comes out shaky. "Are you out there?"

The light filtering in from beneath my door goes off. Then it comes back on. Off and on. Off and on. I scramble out of bed and stand in the corner. A low hiss fills my ears. It drowns out the wind thrashing my window and replaces it with something that sounds less like a hiss and more like a whisper. A snakelike whisper.

Ginnnnny.

Pressing deeper into the corner, I tell myself not to scream. The hiss is coming from the speaking tube, but it isn't Leo this time. I know because my brother would never risk his basketball time to mess with me. Another jagged bolt of lightning flashes. This time when it lights up the mannequin, I gasp. It's no longer facing the bed. It's facing *me*.

The moonlight streaming through my window suddenly fades. The dark swallows my room so fast I can barely breathe. I remember the way the trees had looked as we moved in, like the shadows between their trunks were living, breathing things. This darkness feels the same. Like it's somehow alive.

I stumble toward the door. Part of me wants to look back and see if the mannequin is closer, but the other part of me is too afraid. I flatten my trembling hands on the wall and begin sweeping them side-to-side, desperate to find the doorknob. My fingers finally meet cold metal, but when I turn it nothing happens. I plant my feet and yank as hard as I can, whimpering when the door refuses to open.

"Let me out!" I shriek. "Please!"

Just when I think I'm dead, my door flies open. I scream and jump out of the way. Dad is standing in the hallway, a giant silver candlestick raised above his shoulder like he's about to send my head straight past second base. He's in pajamas and bare feet. His face is pale.

I let out the breath I've been holding. It's not the Hitchhikers. It's just Dad. Dad and a giant candlestick, like a real-life game of Clue.

He lowers the candlestick with trembling hands. His eyes dart wildly around the hallway. "What's going on? Why were you screaming?"

I don't know how to answer that. With my heart still racing, I risk a look behind me. The room looks exactly how it did when I first saw it. The whispering has stopped, and the mannequin is no longer staring at me. Is it possible I was dreaming?

"I heard whispering." The words tumble out before I can stop them.

A flicker of suspicion crosses Dad's face. "Whispers? Coming from the tube again?"

"Yes, but it wasn't Leo this time. The sound was kind of everywhere. Also, the mannequin," I lift a shaking hand and point a finger at it. "It looked different."

A wave of goose bumps breaks out on the back of my neck as I remember the last few minutes. The flickering light under my door. The whispers. The creepy mannequin. It had all seemed so real.

The shocked look on Will's face back at the restaurant pops into my head. He hadn't just looked surprised when I told him we were staying here, he'd looked scared. *For me.*

Dad reaches out and brushes the hair out of my eyes. "Aw, I'm sorry. I know how real nightmares can feel."

"It wasn't a nightmare," I say.

"Well, it wasn't real, either," he answers. Pushing my door open further, he glances at my bedside table where a small stack of my favorite Agatha books is sitting. "Maybe no more of Ms. Christie's books before bed, mmm?"

My cheeks heat up with frustration. "I didn't read tonight. I was too tired."

"Okay," he pats my shoulder. I know he means it to be comforting, but it isn't.

I clench my jaw so hard my teeth hurt. Dad doesn't believe me. Neither will Mom. Sure, I've imagined a few things in the past, like Mr. Goodie. Oh, and the time I thought our mail carrier was actually a spy. But this isn't the same.

Is it?

"Why don't we get back to sleep," Dad suggests, dropping a kiss on the top of my head.

He turns around to walk away, revealing Leo standing in the hallway behind him. His mouth is pressed into a tight line, and his eyes are crinkled with worry. I open my mouth to say it was nothing, but he shakes his head to silence me.

"In the morning." He lumbers back into his room with a drawn-out sigh.

The door snicks shut leaving me in silence again. I make my way back into bed and prop myself up on pillows. My heart rate is slowing down, but my brain is speeding up. I snag my composition notebook from the bedside table, flip on the lamp, and start scratching out thoughts.

- Ticking sound and knock on door—connection?
- Hitchhikers in the woods
- Move mannequin out!

I set the notebook back down on the table, turn off the lamp, and settle beneath my covers. The rain has died down, but I can still hear thunder in the distance. Hopefully the storm won't come back. I don't think I can handle any more scares tonight.

CHAPTER TWELVE

Rubbing my eyes, I peel the blankets off my sticky body. A whole month without air conditioning. *Fun.*

"Ginny?" Leo's hushed voice echoes through my closed door. I consider staying quiet and letting him think I'm still asleep, but the way he looked in the hall last night—like he was actually worried about me—makes me change my mind.

"I'm up. You can come in."

He cracks my door tentatively, his fingers pressed tightly across his eyes. "You're not naked or anything are you?"

I roll my eyes. "No, Leo. I'm not naked."

"That was not a dumb question. It's hot in here!" he says, fanning his red cheeks. "I slept in my underwear so I didn't melt!"

I make a gagging sound. "TMI, Leo. TMI."

He shrugs and smiles. "So...about last night."

I force a blank expression onto my face. "What about it?"

"Oh, please. *You know*. The screaming? You've never had a nightmare like that before, just like you've never gotten carsick before. So, what gives?"

"Nothing! Seriously, when did you get so nosy?" I walk away from him and start rummaging through my clothes for something to wear.

He crosses his arms and scowls. "I've always been nosy. And if you're going to give me a heart attack in the middle of the night, then I deserve to know what's going on."

Exhaling, I turn back around to face him. "Fine. Fine! I got a little...ahh...*spooked* at the restaurant last night. Guess it got under my skin more than I thought it did."

His eyebrows inch together. "Spooked? How?"

"You know that guy I met? Will? He told me some stuff about this house. Scary stuff."

"Ah. About the Hitchhikers?" Leo asks with a chuckle.

"Not exactly," I answer. "We did talk about them a little, yeah, but he said there's other legends...legends about this house."

I look back at the mannequin tucked into the corner. I was too scared to go near it again last night, so it isn't covered. The head is tilted, face staring blankly into the center of the room. I know it's silly, but I feel like it's watching us. Listening to us.

"Earth to Ginny," Leo says, snapping his fingers in front of my face.

"Ugh, stop." I toss the clothes I've chosen onto my messy bed and flop down beside them. "Will said that some people do believe in the Hitchhikers, but that *everyone* is scared of this place."

Leo laughs, then stops when he realizes I'm not joking. "Sorry. But I just can't get over how dumb that name is. *Hitchhikers*, really?"

"Not the point, Leo."

"I know, I know." He clears his throat. "Just that if I were naming something like this, it would be *so* much scarier. Like Murder Clown."

Murder Clown? This is exactly why I don't ask Leo for help when I have problems. If anything, he makes them worse! Like the time I fell asleep with gum in my mouth when I was little and woke up with it stuck in my hair. Leo convinced me we had to cut it out and he should be the one to do it. Six-year-old me believed him. *Big* mistake. I had a bald spot for weeks after that.

"Ugh. Never mind. I should've known better than to talk to you about this."

His face softens. "Dude. Relax. I didn't realize you're really that freaked out. I'll stop joking. But at least tell me what else he said."

"He didn't," I answer with a shrug. "His dad was flipping out, so he had to leave. I can't even google it because my stupid phone doesn't work here at all. Does yours?"

Leo shakes his head. "I tried to watch YouTube last night for a while, but the videos wouldn't even load."

I groan. "This is terrible. First I thought I saw a hand scratching at my window. Then I heard whispering coming from the speaking tube again and the mannequin moved!"

"The mannequin moved," Leo repeats flatly.

"Yes, it moved!" I hiss. "I mean, I thought it did. I was tired, and it all happened so fast. I couldn't get out, though. I *know* I didn't dream that. My door was locked."

His eyes land on the door and narrow. "There's no lock on the door, Gin."

"What?" I jump up and walk over to inspect it. He's right. No lock on the door. "I don't get it."

"Maybe you just thought it was locked. Like, it was stuck or something," he offers.

I guess that's possible. This is an old house, after all.

"Even if that's true, I still think something is weird about this place. I've felt it since the second we walked through

77

the door." I remember the way I'd felt almost immediately...
uncomfortable and anxious. I didn't like it then, and I *really*
don't like it now. "Remember how Dad mentioned that there
might be some rumors about Woodmoor? I'm beginning to
think they're more serious than we thought. Maybe people
don't want to stay here because of them."

Leo nods his head slowly. "And we're stuck here for a
month."

Not if I can help it.

I sigh. "I need to get out of here. I'm gonna see if Mom can
take me into town for a while. Maybe I'll stop at the bookstore
or go look at that typewriter you saw."

"Don't forget snooping around. There's zero chance
you're not going to do that," he quips.

I don't bother to deny it. Agatha Christie would not have
a near-death experience with a faceless mannequin and ignore
it. No, she'd use it to write a wickedly good book. A terrifying
book. A bestseller!

An idea pops into my head. Maybe I could use the things
that happened last night to get back home. If I can prove to
Mom and Dad that the legends around here aren't *just* legends,
I'd get to go home *and* have an incredible idea for my story.
Maybe I could even get back to Chicago in time for the writing
workshop!

I almost pump my fist in the air just thinking about it. Only problem is for all of this to work, the house has to *actually* be cursed or haunted or whatever people around here say. Not gonna lie, that sucks.

Leo heads back to his room. "Well, don't leave without me. I'll go too, maybe shoot some hoops."

That will mean I have to ride all the way back here with a sweaty brother, but at least he'll be in a good mood. He always is when he has a chance to practice.

I nod. "Meet in ten?"

Leo salutes me and walks out, leaving me in silence. Not total silence, of course. I don't think that exists here with the phantom clock ticking away. I snag my composition notebook and shove it in the small backpack I brought with me. Time to get down to business, Ginny Anderson, future *New York Times* bestselling author.

CHAPTER THIRTEEN

"Please?" I beg. Mom originally said no to driving me and Leo into town, but I haven't given up yet. I can't be trapped in this house all day. I can't! "Just for an hour?"

Mom looks at the screen of her phone, then back to me. "I guess so, if we go right now. The weather forecast is for bad storms later this evening, possibly even hail, and I don't want to get caught in that."

More storms? I look out the window uneasily. The sky is cloudy and gray. Bad weather means Woodmoor Manor is going to be even scarier than it already is. I wince at the idea, then refocus on Mom. She's watching me thoughtfully.

"Are you okay, honey? Dad told me about the nightmare you had last night. Must've been awful. You're still pale."

"Am I?" I ask, touching my cheek as if pale skin can

somehow be felt. "Guess I'm just a little tired is all. I didn't sleep well."

She moves her palm to my forehead. "You don't have a fever, do you?"

"Nope." I say this quickly, so she doesn't have second thoughts about letting me go into town. "Anyway, I'm totally ready to go. Leo is too." I take two steps to the doorway of the kitchen and scream, "Leo get down here!"

Mom jumps and covers her ears. "Ginny!"

"Sorry," I say sheepishly. "I just don't want you to change your mind."

"Well, don't worry about that. I already said I would take you, and I will." Mom lifts her keys from the kitchen counter, then pauses and picks up a slip of paper too. "I actually need to go to the store, so maybe I'll do that while you and Leo are busy."

"Okay. Would you mind dropping me off at the bookstore?"

"Pfft. *Nerd*," Leo says as he walks into the room.

My temper flares the way it does every time he starts picking at me for liking to read. Books *aren't* nerdy. Maybe basketballs are nerdy! Or video games! Without thinking, I reach out and fling the closest thing at him. I wish it were a rabid raccoon or a bucket of fish guts, but instead it turns out to be a wicker basket full of...keys? The basket ricochets off my brother. Keys rain down, loudly scattering across the tile floor.

Leo doubles over, laughing hysterically. Meanwhile, Mom looks fed up.

"Sorry, I got 'em!" I drop down to my hands and knees and begin quickly picking up the keys. I really didn't think that through. I was definitely ahead on the Leo versus Ginny scorecard earlier, thanks to his speaking tube prank, but now we might be tied.

As I'm shoving them all back into the basket, I pick up a particularly strange looking one and hold it up in the air. One end is a circle and the other end is squarish with two points sticking out like teeth. The stem in between the two ends is long, much longer than a normal key. I flip it over and back again, deciding it's something called a skeleton key. I've read about them before but have never seen one in real life. Apparently, they're hollow on the inside and were made to open many different doors instead of just one. I snort, thinking that the janitor at my school needs one. Maybe then he wouldn't have to haul around a key ring with dozens of keys on it all the time.

"What are you doing?" Leo huffs. "I thought we were in *such* a big hurry." He waves his hands around in the air, mimicking chaos.

I focus on ignoring him as I gently set the basket back on the counter. Placing the skeleton key on top of the others, I can't help but wish I knew more about it. It reminds me of something one of Agatha's characters would research. Maybe they'd even prowl around the house with it, testing doors so they can find out what it leads to.

Scratch that. Testing that key is something *I* should do. I wait until Mom and Leo walk out of the kitchen, then I grab the key and shove it into my shorts pocket. I don't know what it opens yet, but I will.

Even with the gray skies, downtown Saugatuck is still cute. Families dot the sidewalks, pushing strollers and playing with dogs. A few groups of kids my age walk past, chattering excitedly as they lick at rapidly melting ice cream cones. I wish I could be happy like that. Carefree, like my biggest problem is if I can get my rocky road snarfed down before the sun turns it into chocolate goo.

Mom drops off Leo first. The basketball court is small, nothing more than a patch of concrete with faded lines painted on it and two hoops at each end. There are five or six kids already playing but knowing my brother that won't matter. I'm not jealous of much when it comes to Leo, but the way he makes friends so fast is cool. He can be anywhere and just start talking to someone.

"Here you are. I'll call you when I'm done with my errands," Mom says, pulling the car over in front of the bookstore.

I look down at my phone, relieved to see there's reception here. Must be better in town. I immediately text Erica again—hi, miss you—smiling when it goes through.

"Okay, thanks."

I hop out of the car. The air is sweet here. Better than Woodmoor, which always smells a little like my grandma Annie's house. She has five cats. Mom and Dad have tried to get her to give a few of them to us even though we really don't want any cats, but she refuses. Says they're her babies. Too bad the babies make all her furniture smell like pee.

Stepping into the bookstore, I gasp. It's *awesome*. If I wasn't so worried about what happened to me at Woodmoor last night, I'd definitely be looking for the owner. But I can't. Not yet. I need to straighten out some things first.

I step in further and inhale the best scent in the world—books. There's a whole section of shiny, new releases to my left, and to my right, a shelf of the "classics." My eyes immediately land on a copy of *And Then There Were None*. I pick it up and crack it open, reminded of the first time I read that story. It was my first Agatha Christie book, and I loved it from page one. Soldier Island, a series of deaths, lots of suspects...it's perfect. I'm just about to ease down to the floor so I can read a few pages when a familiar voice stops me.

"Hey. Ginny, right?"

I look up to see the boy from the restaurant smiling at me. What's he doing here?

"Yeah. Hi."

"You an Agatha Christie fan?" he asks, watching as I fumble to get the book back onto the shelf.

"I am. I like all mystery novels, really, but she's my favorite." I watch as Will reaches out and plucks the copy of *And Then There Were None* off the shelf and resituates it in a different spot. Um, okay. Erica has this thing about items in her room being even, like if there are two pictures on one wall there have to be two pictures on the other walls too. It took me a while to get used to it, but now it's totally normal. Maybe Will is like that?

As if he can read my mind, he laughs and says, "I work here. I mean, it's more like an internship since I don't get paid, but next summer I'll be old enough to be employed here for real."

My mouth falls open. Will *works* here? I can't tell if I'm jealous or impressed. Maybe a little of both.

He points to the book he just moved. "The owner, Greta, is really weird about how series are arranged on the shelves. Likes the books to be in order of when they first released."

"Oh. Um, does she know you can read her books out of order?" I ask. "I mean, she's so good at describing her characters that you can pick up any of them first and still totally understand."

Will smirks. "Wow. You really do like her, huh?"

Even though he's smirking, it isn't a mean kind of smirk. It's playful, like he understands. Does he understand? He works at a bookstore, after all. Maybe Will is like me, into books and writing and stuff.

"So, why did you want to work here? Isn't there like an ice-cream shop on this street?" I ask the question because a good mystery writer always looks for something called motive. What makes people do what they do. Why would Will work at a bookstore when Saugatuck seems to have so many other choices? Even though I know I shouldn't get my hopes up, I wonder if it's possible he actually likes to read.

"I like it here. It's quiet, and I can actually read in between customers."

I can't fight the smile that breaks out on my face. "You like to read?"

He looks surprised. "Doesn't everyone?"

"My brother calls me a nerd for reading as much as I do. So, no. Not really." I laugh awkwardly.

Will looks disappointed at this. "Well, I think *he's* the nerd. I want to do something with books someday. Like work at one of those big publishing companies. You know, be the person who finds the next big thing!"

"We have something in common, then," I tell him.

"You want to find the next big thing too?"

"No," I answer, grinning. "I want to *be* the next big thing."

Will bursts into laughter. A few people milling around the back of the store look at us. He slaps a hand over his mouth. After a few seconds, he finally removes it and starts tugging me deeper into the store. "In that case, follow me. Something arrived at the store this morning that I think you'll want to see."

CHAPTER FOURTEEN

A typewriter is sitting on a small table in a room at the back of the store. I gasp, wondering if it's the same one Leo saw.

"The typewriter! Wasn't this at the antique shop?"

Will looks confused. "Wait, you've seen this before?"

"No, but my brother did. He said it was in the window of an antique shop down the street." I take a few steps closer and run my fingers over the cool metal. It's exactly like the one I've always wanted. The buttons are all there and the paint is still in perfect condition. It hardly even looks used!

"Hmm. I never noticed it there. This is the first time I've seen it."

Weird.

I nervously glance back at the door that leads into the main bookstore area. "Is it okay that we're doing this right now? I don't want you to miss anyone shoplifting out there."

"Shoplifting?" Will asks with a mischievous grin. "Where are you from, anyway? Let me guess... Chicago?"

"How did you know that?"

"A lot of people who come here for vacation are from Chicago. Plus, my older sister is in college there. DePaul. Her bike got stolen on campus the very first week!"

I make a sour face and tell him that stinks. Stuff *does* get stolen in Chicago a lot. I never leave my bike anywhere without a lock on it, and once, even with that, someone took my back tire. Just the tire! Who does that?

"So, you're *not* from Chicago?" I ask.

"Nope. Ann Arbor. It's in Michigan. We have a college there too." He points to the blue M on the front of his T-shirt. "University of Michigan. Go Blue!"

I pump my fist in the air awkwardly even though I really don't know anything about the University of Michigan. Or any universities, really. I look Will up and down, wondering if he's my age.

"And no," Will continues. "We aren't going to get into trouble. Greta is on a coffee break, and Lilian is working in the store with me. She's in high school and has worked here a long time, so she's fine alone for a minute."

I touch the keys of the typewriter gently, imagining what it would feel like to type *The End* with it. Fantastic, I think. "What is Greta going to do with this?"

He shrugs. "No clue. Maybe she bought it from the antique shop and is going to display it out in the store or something? It *would* look cool."

My stomach sinks. If Greta bought the typewriter for herself, then I don't have a chance at owning it. Not that I have the money anyway, but still.

I notice there's a piece of paper loaded into the machine. Even though it's probably just for show, there's a word typed onto it in bold, black ink.

GET.

I stare at the letters, wondering who started to type on this machine and what they were going to say. Leo used to do this thing every time we went into a store that sold computers or phones where he'd type his name on all the screens and leave them that way. Seems dumb, but maybe someone did that same thing with this typewriter. Only instead of their name, they started to write part of their grocery list. *Get apples. Get butter. Get lettuce.* I don't know. People are strange.

Taking a step back from the typewriter, I meet Will's eyes. "Hey. Remember when we met in the restaurant?"

He snorts. "You mean the fire hazard? Yup. How's your toe, by the way?"

I smile. He has a good memory. "It's fine. Thanks. But... um... I wanted to ask you a question about something you said."

"Okay. What's up?"

"It's about Woodmoor. The house I'm staying in."

Will's expression changes. It's wary now, like he's uncomfortable talking about this. "What about it? Did something happen?"

"Kinda," I admit. "I mean, I don't know for sure. I might have dreamed it."

He takes in a deep breath, then says, "I'm going to ask Lilian if I can take a break. We can go somewhere else and talk."

Peeking around the room, I shrug. "I guess, but what's wrong with here?"

"Greta works part-time at the historical society. She's really into the history of the towns around here. But she also gets super offended when people talk about the legends." He scoffs. "Last week a film crew came here from one of those ghost hunter shows on TV, and she got *so* mad. Said it's disrespectful to the people and real history of these towns to talk about 'such nonsense.'"

"So, if she came back and overheard us, she'd be mad?" I ask.

"Totally," he confirms. "Hold on. I'll be right back."

Will walks through the door back into the main part of the store. While he's gone, I draw closer to the typewriter again. I know I shouldn't, but I want to type on it. Just one letter. I look back to the door, listening for footsteps or any clue that Will is coming back, and when I get nothing but silence, I do it. I press the *g*.

The little metal part flips up, hits the paper, and leaves behind...nothing. No *g*. Huh. I try it again, this time a little harder in case you have to do that with these things. As much as I want a typewriter, I've never actually had the chance to use one.

When the *g* doesn't appear again, I bend down and look into the machine. Maybe it's out of ink? Possible, but then how did someone type the word *get*? An idea pops into my head. Perhaps a person typed that word a really long time ago and the antique store just left the paper in, hoping people would believe the typewriter works so they buy it? Ha. If that's true, then the people who own the antique store are kinda jerks.

Will comes back into the room. "Okay! All set."

"Hey, does your boss know this doesn't work?" I point at the typewriter.

"It doesn't?" he asks, leaning in to look at it closer. "But there's the word typed on it."

"I know. I just tried it, though, and *nothing*."

"Hope she didn't spend much on it, then. It's cool and all, but if it doesn't work it's not worth much."

I nod like I agree, but deep down I don't. In fact, I'm hoping that Will tells Greta the typewriter is broken, and she decides to get rid of it. Then maybe I could buy it. Except there's the money thing. I only have thirty bucks. Total. And if his boss bought it as a display item, maybe she won't even care if it doesn't work.

"Ready to go?" Will asks, holding open the door.

I follow him out, only partly ready to explain what happened last night in my room at Woodmoor. I'm even less ready to hear what Will has to say about it. If the expression on his face was any clue, then I'm in for some scary stuff. Hopefully it's enough to get me one step closer to going back home.

CHAPTER FIFTEEN

Will takes me to an ice-cream shop! It's enormous and has a man in the front window actually making the fudge while people watch. I stare, mesmerized, as he pours the hot chocolate out of a large bowl and onto a marble table. The table must be cold because he uses a scraper to start moving around the chocolate, which is already getting solid on the bottom. My mouth waters.

"Tell me what you want, and I'll get it. You grab a table."

"Cool." I start digging in my bag for money, but Will holds up a hand.

"See that guy up there? The one at the register?"

I look up and see a fluffy-haired boy around my brother's age. He's wearing a dorky hat that says *Eat More Chocolate* and is smiling as he gives an older woman her change. "Yeah? Why?"

"That's Craig. My brother," Will says, giving a little wave in his direction.

I look back at Craig. Now that Will told me they're brothers, I see the resemblance. Although Craig has darker hair than Will, their eyes are the same bright blue.

"Anyway," Will continues. "I get the family discount here." He winks exaggeratedly and I laugh. Apparently, family discount means free.

"Okay. If you're sure. Could I get candy instead of ice cream? Maybe one of those round turtles? The ones with the—"

"Caramel and nuts?" Will finishes for me. I give him a thumbs-up and he says, "Those are my favorite. Be right back."

Chocolate turtles are his favorite. Another thing we have in common.

Will returns to the table a few minutes later. He has a paper bag in his hand. "Two turtles and a peanut butter cup to share." He uses a plastic knife to split the extra piece. "You aren't allergic to peanut butter, are you? Please say no because these things are *really* good."

"No," I say, gratefully taking my half and sinking my teeth into it. Ho-ly cow. Will wasn't kidding. It's incredible.

"So," he says around a mouthful of chocolate. "What's going on?"

"It's not that big of a deal," I answer, even though that's not true. What happened in my room last night *was* a big deal. It was scary. "I just heard some things in my room last night."

"Like what?"

"Whispering, mainly. The storm woke me up and that's when I started hearing it. I also thought I saw the mannequin that's sitting in my corner...*move*." Heat rises into my cheeks. Admitting this is more embarrassing than I thought it would be. Even though Will isn't acting like I'm bananas, I wouldn't blame him if he did.

Will leans back in his chair and sets the other half of his turtle down on a napkin. "First of all, they're making you sleep in a room with a mannequin in it?"

"Yes. And it doesn't even have a face!"

He blows out a long breath, clearly bothered. "That sucks. And you can't move it?"

I roll my shoulders. "Not sure, but I'm going to ask when I get back home. Thing is, my dad is super into history, and he doesn't like messing with anything that's an antique."

"Ah. My dad doesn't care about history, but he really cares about our thermostat because he doesn't like anyone touching that. '*The bill will just skyrocket,*'" he mimics.

I laugh. Even if I don't find out much from Will today, I'm

glad I came. He's funny. And nice. He's also better than a faceless mannequin and a terrifying speaking tube, so there's that.

"Back at the restaurant, you said there are other legends— legends about Woodmoor. What were you talking about?"

Something dark flickers in his expression. "The Shadow People. I don't know much, really, but I've heard little bits and pieces about the legend since I started coming here when I was six. Apparently, a lot of people who have visited or stayed at Woodmoor Manor have left in a *big* hurry because they saw or heard something. Scary shadows mainly. Sometimes they have glowing eyes." He stops abruptly and meets my eyes. "Do you believe in that kind of stuff? Curses and ghosts and all that?"

Do I? Before coming here, I think I would have said no. I've never seen or heard anything unexplainable before. In the books I read, there's usually a good explanation for the mysterious happenings. Even in stories like *Murder on the Orient Express*, where the perfect, footprint-free snow around the trapped train might make it seem like the murder is impossible to solve, it's not. Agatha has an explanation. She always does.

But this? This is different. I'm not trying to solve a murder, and I don't have any real suspects. I've only got legends— legends that might be nothing more than the campfire stories Dad claims they are.

"Is it weird if I say I don't know if I believe in it? I mean, it sounds silly, but last night felt real. And my door was locked too. My door that *doesn't have a lock*. I forgot to tell you that. I couldn't get out."

"Did you see any shadows?" he asks pointedly.

I shake my head. "Nope. There is a connection though, because right before I went to my room, we had to carry some boxes into storage."

"And?"

"And the storage was in the ballroom. The ballroom *you* told me to stay away from."

His mouth drops open. "Well, that could be a coincidence I guess."

I narrow my eyes on him. The crack in Will's voice gave him away. He doesn't think it was a coincidence at all. I set down the last bit of my turtle, suddenly very un-hungry.

"Why did you say that I should stay away from the ballroom?" I press. "Was that because people have reported seeing the Shadow People up there?" Dragging out my notebook, I start jotting down some thoughts. I need to keep good notes if I'm going to present all this to Mom and Dad later. Proving we should go home won't be easy.

Will nods reluctantly. "Yeah. The couple that runs the bed-and-breakfast down the street love creepy things. One time they came into the store looking for books on Saugatuck history. The lady was *obsessed* with Woodmoor. She told me that when people take pictures in the ballroom, sometimes they'll end up seeing a person in the photo who wasn't in the room with them. Or they see shadows lurking in the corner."

"Are they dangerous?"

He pauses, then nods warily. "If the Shadow People are responsible for all the bad things I've heard of happening at Woodmoor, maybe. Cars that were fine when people arrived won't start when they leave. Doors open and close on their own. The power goes off for no reason. That kind of thing."

It's probably just because it's chilly in the ice-cream shop, but suddenly I'm cold. My teeth chatter together, and I fold my arms over each other for warmth. "Do *you* believe that stuff?"

Will is silent for a long moment. When he finally speaks, it sends a jolt of fear through me. "I have to believe it. I've seen them."

CHAPTER SIXTEEN

I have a witness.

I quickly scribble Will's name down in my notebook. Turning my attention back to him, I tap my pen impatiently against the paper as I wait for more.

He nervously runs a hand through his hair. "I know. I know. I should have told you right away, but I was little when it happened. Like eight, maybe? I don't even know if I'm remembering it right."

Funny, that's exactly how I felt when I woke up this morning. The events of last night were blurry and unfocused. Like maybe they'd all been nothing more than a dream...

"It was one of our first few summers coming here. We didn't stay the whole time back then, only a couple weeks." He glances at his brother, who is dumping scoops of chocolate covered pretzels into a bag for someone. "Mom and Dad were thinking of buying a place here, so they wanted us to explore the area more than just floating around on a lake for eight hours a day. They ended up taking us on a tour through Woodmoor Manor.

"When we got to the house, everyone just kind of split up," he says, blinking hard at the memory. "I ended up with Craig while Mom and Dad got hung up in the library oohing and aahing over the old pictures."

"Wait, I thought it was a tour. Why were you guys separated?"

"I don't know how their tours run now, but back then, someone gave you a brochure when you arrived and talked for a minute about the house. Then you just looked around on your own."

I make a note of that, then motion for him to go on. I can't help but notice how pale his face is now, like just telling this story is scaring him all over again.

"Anyway, Craig and I went upstairs. We found the ballroom. It was the only space big enough for us to throw Craig's foam football back and forth, so that's what we did. I made a bad throw, and it flew into a corner where some boxes were stacked. Craig went to get it."

I'm sitting on the edge of my seat. Literally. I know Will

doesn't want to be a writer, but he sure does have a way of telling stories.

"Craig stopped a few feet away from the boxes and just stood there. He was so still, like he was frozen. I couldn't figure out why he wasn't getting the ball, so I walked over to him." Will stops to take a breath. His hands are shaking. "I'll never forget the look on his face. His eyes were *huge*, and his mouth was wide open like he was trying to scream."

I lick my lips, suddenly very afraid of what Will is about to say. "What was it?"

"That's just it. I don't know for sure."

"What do you mean you don't know? You said you've seen the Shadow People!"

"Okay, I said that wrong. I didn't see them, but Craig did. I know he did."

I realize I've been absentmindedly scribbling a random pattern on my page and stop. "Did he tell you that?"

"He didn't have to," Will says. "I know my brother. He was terrified. He ran out of the ballroom without even taking his football, which was like his prized possession back then."

I almost throw my notebook at his forehead. "This doesn't prove anything, Will. Craig could have seen a big spider or something."

He shakes his head violently. "No. It wasn't a spider. Craig saw something scary in that house. Besides, that's not exactly the end of it."

I set my pen down, unsure how to feel about all of this. Sharing this experience seems draining to Will. Almost like he's having to relive it all over again. And based on his pale face and shaky hands, it was bad enough the first time. He might not have seen a Shadow Person firsthand, but he still had a bad experience in the house. That's definitely something Mom and Dad would want to know. Right?

"Craig took off. He just...left me. I was terrified. So, I chased after him. Just as I reached the bottom of the stairs, a blast of cold air hit me." Will looks up, his lips set into a thin, white line. When he finally speaks again, it sends a chill up the back of my neck. "Someone was watching me. I couldn't see them, but I could *feel* them."

Cupping the back of his neck with a palm, he laughs feebly. "Sounds totally made up, right?"

Yes. But a moving mannequin does too, so...

"Anyway, I ran straight down the stairs, past my parents, and out of the house. I've never been back," he finishes.

"I'm sorry that happened to you." I finally say, closing my notebook. As much as I want proof for my presentation to Mom and Dad, and evidence for the story I'll write on Woodmoor when I get back to Chicago, I don't want to be mean to Will.

A faint smile curves his lips upward. "It's okay. I haven't really thought about it in a while. Until you showed up."

I cringe. "I'm sorry I brought back bad memories for you."

"You didn't. Not really." He wads up our used napkins and stuffs them into the bag. "Anyway, now you know why I was so freaked out about you staying at Woodmoor. I haven't been back there since the...*incident*."

The incident. The one that doesn't seem to share any similarities with what happened to me. No whispers, no moving mannequin, no locked doors. I still think it means something, though. It has to.

"Don't you want to know what Craig saw? Maybe now that you guys are older you could ask him?"

"I've tried. He doesn't want to talk about it."

Maybe Will isn't asking the right way. Or asking the right questions. In Agatha's books, Hercule Poirot is a detective. He's really good at solving mysteries, mostly because he's good at figuring people out. I'd love a chance to figure Craig out.

I look down at my phone, realizing with a jolt that I've missed five calls from Mom. I turned my ringer down in the bookstore because loud phones when you're trying to pick out a new book are annoying. I must have forgotten to turn it back up.

Frantically texting her a message, I notice Leo has been texting me too.

Where r u?

Mom is mad.

Dude. Seriously.

Giving Will an apologetic look, I jump up and toss our trash in the bin. "I gotta go."

Will stands. "I overshared, didn't I?"

"No! It's not that. I missed a bunch of calls from my mom, and now she and my brother are both pretty unhappy with me. They're parked back down by the bookstore."

"I'll walk you back," Will offers.

"Wanna jog me back instead?" I ask, only partly joking. Mom doesn't get mad about much, but she really hates it when we don't answer our phones or keep her updated about where we are. I think it's another side effect of living in a big city. Chicago is great and all, but it's busy and things happen. Mom just doesn't want them to happen to us.

Will and I walk out the door together, my stomach in knots. Nothing he told me lines up with what happened to me, and even if it did, I'm not sure I feel good about pressing him about it again. I don't think Agatha would, either.

CHAPTER SEVENTEEN

"We were worried sick!" Mom exclaims. Again. "First day in a new town and you turn your phone on silent? Honestly, Ginny. I almost called the police!"

"I'm sorry," I say, even though it didn't matter the first five times. Mom has been doing this since I got in the car, Leo smirking in the passenger seat beside her. Every time I catch a glimpse of his face in the rearview mirror, he's wearing the same smug smile. It makes me want to throw the basket of keys at him all over again.

The key. I touch my shorts pocket, breathing a sigh of relief when I feel the outline of the skeleton key. I still don't know what it might unlock, but I need to keep it safe. I run through a list of places to hide it in my head, finally settling on my suitcase. It's empty, so no one should have any reason to look inside it.

A crack of thunder overhead makes me jump. The once gray skies are turning black and ugly, like a scene out of some disaster movie. I'd give anything not to be going back to Woodmoor Manor right now. I'd also give anything to know how what happened to Will's brother and what happened to me are connected. They don't look like they are, but if I've learned one thing from Agatha's novels, it's that things aren't always as they seem.

I glance down at my phone, wishing Will would text me. He'd asked for my phone on the way back to the car so he could put his number in it. I wish I could hide out in the bookstore today. It could storm all it wants, but I'd be safe, snuggled in a pile of books. I'd also be around Will, which I've discovered I kinda like.

"Both of you grab a bag or two from the trunk to carry in, please," Mom says, slamming the car into park. She's apparently gonna be upset with me for a while. "I'm very behind on starting dinner now."

She doesn't say "because of Ginny," but I know that's what she means. "It won't happen again, Mom," I promise.

Mom harrumphs and grabs a bag overflowing with baking supplies. I lift one that looks more like a dinner ingredients bag. I see cilantro on top, which is a great sign. Mom never makes anything with cilantro except for guacamole, and that's one of my favorite foods.

A gust of wind rips across the lawn. It's cold and smells a little like lake water. I speed up just as the first drops of rain begin hitting my bare shoulders. A flash of lightening brightens the treetops and makes my heart beat faster. I'm not afraid of storms. Not in Chicago, anyway. Woodmoor is different, though.

"Ginny, hurry up!" Mom is at the front door, waving me toward her. I move faster, the wind howling around me. It almost sounds like someone's crying.

By the time I reach the front door, my entire tank top is drenched, and my hair is dripping. I stop in the lobby, panting. "How long is this supposed to last?"

Dad takes the bag from my hands. "A few hours, unfortunately. The front is just moving in, and it's big."

Great. I slide the hair tie off my wrist and use it to pull my soggy curls up into a messy knot on my head. Better than having it drip down my back. "I'm going to go change clothes."

"Good idea," Dad says. Hmmm. He's in a good mood, which means Mom probably hasn't had time to tell him about me turning my phone down yet. I stop with one foot on the stair. "Hey, would it be okay if we move the mannequin out of my room?"

Dad looks at me quizzically. "Why?"

"It's kind of creepy," I say truthfully. The mannequin *is* creepy and anyone other than him would think that.

"I suppose I can see that. I'd like to say yes, but I've promised we won't touch any of the display items. Remember? A lot of them are already in storage in preparation for the renovations, so moving anything additional might confuse the system they already have going." He shifts the grocery bag into his other arm. "Plus, it's affixed to the floor."

I must look confused, because he chuckles. "*Stuck.* The mannequin is permanently attached to the floor."

My mind flashes back to last night. The mannequin *wasn't* attached to the floor. It looked like it was pulled out of the corner, facing me. I shiver at the memory.

"Ginny?" Dad prompts. "You're shaking like a leaf. Why don't we talk about the mannequin later? You go get changed before you catch a cold."

I start to walk away when the unfairness of it all hits me. "But why would they attach it to the floor? Shouldn't they let people who are staying in that room decide whether or not to have that *thing* in there with them?"

Dad's head tips slightly to one side as if he's considering my question. "First of all, the mannequin is probably attached to the floor so that people don't accidentally knock it over and damage the ball gown. Second of all, you seem really upset about this. Any chance it has something to do with the nightmare you had last night?"

Wind roars against the front door, and the lights flicker a few times. The invisible ticking clock echoes in my ears. I fight off another round of shivers and look up the dark stairwell, dread beginning to build. Dry clothes are in my room. I'll have to go up there eventually.

I realize I've been holding my breath again, so I let it out and shake my head. "Like I said, I just think it's creepy is all."

Normally I don't keep secrets from Mom and Dad. But I know exactly what will happen if I tell them what's actually going on without being able to prove it. They'll tell me I'm imagining it, that I've read too many mystery books or that I've lost control of my imagination again. No. I need to be prepared. I need evidence, solid proof they can't question or ignore.

Dad nods, but his face tells a different story. He looks unconvinced. I toss him a smile, hoping that helps.

"No more stalling. Go get changed. I'm going to go help your mother with dinner, then get a little work done. Tomorrow is filled with meetings I need to be ready for."

I take a step up and stop. "Meetings with who?"

"Oh, the manager of the estate, the historical society, things like that."

The historical society. Interesting. I don't know exactly what they do, but I bet they have a lot of information about this house. That's probably why Dad is meeting with them to begin with. Maybe if I went along, I could learn something helpful. "Can I go?"

"What? Why would you want to do that?" Dad asks with a chuckle. "I don't think listening to me discuss renovations to tiles and woodwork sounds like the best you can do with a summer day on vacation."

Vacation. Ha.

"I think it would be interesting. So, can I?"

Dad considers my question. Just when I think he might say yes, he shakes his head. "I don't think that's the best idea, Gin. Not yet. I've never met these people in person, and Monday will be very important for setting the tone. I should be in full business mode, not Dad mode."

My shoulders sag. Whatever. I don't need the historical society. I'll find a way to get my own research done tomorrow.

CHAPTER EIGHTEEN

I'm savoring the feeling of warm, dry sweatpants and a pair of fluffy socks when my phone dings.

Did your mom kill you?

It's a text from Will. I smile and text him back, Not yet. But she's mad.

It takes forever for my text to go through this time. Then I wait for what feels like an eternity for Will to respond. Finally, the little dots pulse on my screen, telling me he's texting back. Hope that wasn't my fault.

Nope, I respond. Totally mine. Don't worry about it.

I don't want Will to feel bad about what happened today. I mean it when I say it wasn't his fault. I was concentrating and lost track of time. Mom and Dad have always said that when I get focused on something, the rest of the world just fades away. Like reading a good book. It's impossible to stop, so sometimes I'll read straight through dinner or late into the night. I can't help it.

You busy tomorrow?

I think on this, unsure how to answer him. I'd like to hang out. Only problem is I really need to get some research done too. I want to find out more about the Shadow People and also see if there are any doors here in Woodmoor that the skeleton key will open. I also want to take another shot at finding the clock.

An idea hatches in my brain. If I could convince Will to come here again, he could research with me. He seems like the kind of guy who might be good at that sort of thing. Plus, this could be his chance to figure out what Craig *really* saw that day in the ballroom.

I have to do some research. Wanna come here and help?

The little dots pulse and stop. Pulse and stop. Then they just...stop. Ugh. I never should have asked him. Will made it pretty clear that he's hated this place since the scary experience with his brother. Of course he doesn't want to come back here.

My phone finally dings again. Okay.

Really?

Will responds, Yeah but no ballroom.

Deal, I respond, then set my phone down. I'll figure out when we're meeting tomorrow. Right now, I want to get back downstairs with the rest of my family. Being alone up here isn't fun. The rain is lashing at the windows even harder than before, and each flash of lightning sends a different, gnarled shape across my floor.

I look bitterly at the mannequin. Dumb display item. If they wanted to show off that ball gown without being creepy, they should have just put it on a hanger! My eyes travel down to the base of it. The ball gown is so long it pools onto the floor. If it is anchored to the ground, I can't see what they used. Doesn't matter, I guess. Dad said we aren't allowed to move it. I'll just have to do the next best thing.

Snatching up the blanket I used to cover it before, I get close enough to toss it over the head again. I keep several feet between my body and the mannequin as I swing the blanket up and over. It drapes across the right half of the figure, but the entire left side is still showing. Not good enough. I take another tiny step closer and try to rearrange it. With just a few tugs to the left, it should cover the whole thing and I won't have to look at it anymore. Instead, I'll have a ghostly blanket-covered blob in the corner of my room.

Blah.

I've almost got the mannequin completely covered when a sharp crack pierces the silence. More thunder. My windows rattle and the lights flicker.

Once.

Twice.

Three times.

Then...they go out. I'm frozen in place, too afraid to move. A scream echoes up from downstairs. Mom! What's happening down there? I stumble in the direction I *think* the door is in but stop when I crash into the bathroom sink. Wrong way.

Stifling a sob, I turn around and feel my way back out into the bedroom. Another bolt of lightning breaks through the darkened sky. It brightens my room long enough for me to see the bed and my phone. If I can just make it over there, I can use the flashlight on it to get out of here!

A series of thuds from the corner of my room makes my heart speed up. I whirl in that direction. There's a scuffling sound now, like something moving. My imagination runs wild with the thought of the mannequin crawling across my floor. It's so dark that it could be right in front of me for all I know! Breaking into a sprint, I launch myself onto the bed and frantically feel around for my phone. I need that flashlight *now.*

My hands are shaking so hard I can barely hold onto the phone once I find it. I swipe down on the screen and turn on the flashlight. Swinging it from side to side, I look at my room. At first, it looks normal. Then a streak of something tells me it's most definitely not.

A shadow.

It hovers by the blanket-covered mannequin, then slithers past the fireplace and into the sunroom on a wisp of blueish-black. It's edges ripple and curl like smoke drifting off a campfire, but with each flutter, my room feels colder. When the shadow reaches the window, it just...vanishes.

The lights hum loudly for a moment, then flick back on. I'm in the center of my bed, shaking and crying and completely lost. My room is so cold that each breath I release comes out a puff of white.

They're real.

The Shadow People are real, and they're here.

CHAPTER NINETEEN

"Mom!" I scream, racing out of my room and down the hall on wobbly legs.

I take the stairs two at a time, hoping I can get down to the first floor safely before the lights cut out again. The wind slams into Woodmoor over and over, howling and thrashing at the windows like an angry monster. I can't stop looking behind me, terrified that at any moment the shadow will appear on my heels.

Sweat drips down my forehead. I had almost convinced myself I dreamed the things that happened in my room last night. Not anymore. That shadow was real and so are the rumors about this horrible house.

Sliding into the kitchen, I skid to a stop by the refrigerator. Mom immediately holds up both hands, palms facing me. "Don't come any closer, Gin!"

I blink at her, confused. "What? Why?"

Dad rises from behind the counter. He's got a handful of something clear and jagged. "Light bulb exploded. Two, actually."

"There's glass everywhere, so stay back. I don't want to have to drive anyone to the emergency room tonight." Mom shuffles a few feet to grab a broom and dustpan. "How did this even happen?"

Dad drops the glass fragments into a trash bag and sighs. "I'm not sure. The electric isn't that old in this house. They redid it with the first set of renovations. Light bulbs shouldn't be exploding like that."

I bite my tongue to keep from saying what I want to say, that the light bulbs exploding has nothing to do with the electricity and everything to do with the evil in this house. The Shadow People. I blink back the tears I can feel building.

"Oh, honey. It's okay." Mom carefully sidesteps the glass and draws closer to me. She wraps her arms around my shoulders and squeezes. "It's just a summer storm and some bad wires."

"It's not," I sniffle, then clamp my mouth shut. I *really* want to blurt out everything to Mom and Dad right now. Tell them about the whispers, the lights, the mannequin, and the shadow. But that would be a bad idea. *I'm* the one who didn't want to come here. *I'm* the one who made a big fuss about it and tried to convince them to stay in Chicago. I can't be the witness in this mystery... It would look fishy. Convenient. *Made up.*

No. Mom and Dad can't hear about the bad things at Woodmoor Manor from me. Not if I want them to believe it. They need to hear it from someone who will tell the truth because they don't have any reason to lie.

They need to hear it from Craig.

If I can get Craig to talk about what he saw all those years ago, then prove I've had the same experience, they'll let us go home for sure. I swipe at the tears running down my face, then look around the room, noticing my brother isn't here. "Where's Leo?"

"In his room. Sleeping, maybe?"

At five thirty? No way. Leo is what my parents call a night owl. He likes to stay up late. There's zero chance he's asleep right now.

I jog out of the kitchen and head toward the stairwell. In my mind, I imagine Leo backed against a wall in his room. His eyes are wide, his mouth open in the same silent scream as Craig.

I take a steadying breath at the bottom of the steps, then tell myself now is not the time to be a chicken. I need to make sure Leo is okay. He would do the same for me.

"Leo?" I call out as I reach the landing with the little wooden bench. The giant window above me reveals rivers of rain and deep, black clouds. "Are you up here?"

No response, other than the persistent tick, tick, ticking of the clock.

I creep up the last few steps, my legs quaking so hard it's difficult to stay balanced. The lights flicker once more, making me hesitate. I don't want to get trapped in the dark up here again. But Leo...he could be in trouble. I'm not sure what the Shadow People are capable of, but they aren't trying to be my friends so far. That's for sure.

Leo's door is shut. I think I can hear music coming from inside, but it's hard to tell with the thunder constantly rumbling. I don't bother knocking. I turn the handle, grit my teeth together, and walk in.

CHAPTER TWENTY

Leo is standing in front of the mirrored dresser. Music is coming from a small wireless speaker sitting on the bed. He's dancing, flailing around to the music as he lip-synchs into a shampoo bottle like it's a microphone.

A laugh bubbles free. Leo startles and spins around. "Ginny! What... What are you doing in here? Why didn't you knock?" His cheeks redden.

"Sorry, I was checking on you. I didn't know you were putting on a talent show up here." I break into another round of laughter. The way he'd been dancing around was hilarious. No wonder he didn't hear all the ruckus in the house. Between the music, the thunder, and his thick door, he couldn't.

Leo sets the bottle down and scowls. "Don't come in here without knocking again. I could have been changing clothes!"

"Or just dancing really, *really* badly," I tease.

The redness in his cheeks creeps up a notch as he turns the speaker off. I'd feel bad about taunting him, but this is too good. Plus, I *might* still be looking for revenge for the speaking tube thing.

"Shut up," Leo spits out. "What do you want, anyway? Seriously."

Suddenly, I remember why I came up here and the lip-synching isn't as funny. "Some weird things were happening, and Mom and Dad didn't know where you were, so—"

"Wait," he interrupts. "Were you *worried* about me?"

"No!" I immediately fire back.

He folds his arms over his chest and smiles. "Right. You still think there's something going on in this house, don't you? You came up here to save me from it."

The tone in his voice is irritating. I toss my hands in the air and say, "Forget it, then. If I'd known you'd be a jerk about it, I would have just let it eat you."

"Let *what* eat me?"

"The Shadow Person!" I hiss. "Maybe you didn't notice the lights going out, but they did, and it showed up in my room."

Leo's face is grave. "What?"

"A few minutes ago, a shadowy *thing* creeped through

my room. Light bulbs burst in the kitchen over Mom's and Dad's heads too." I wring my clammy hands together, my heart fluttering like a scared butterfly all over again. "Dad can't explain it, but I think I can. The Shadow People are real."

He lowers to a seat on his bed. "It's an old house, Ginny. We knew it would be broken down from the start. The light bulbs, the sounds, the darkness... It's probably all just more stuff Dad needs to tell them to renovate."

"No. It's more than that. Like I said, I saw it. It moved across my room and made everything cold. I could see my breath!"

When he still looks unconvinced, I sit next to him. "Dad said the mannequin in my room is attached to the floor. But last night, it was in a different spot in my room. It moved, Leo. Then my door without a lock was suddenly locked? How are these things possible?"

"I don't know," he admits wearily. "Maybe you're right. Maybe all this unexplained stuff has something to do with the rumors."

"It does," I say firmly. "And I'm not the only one who has seen things in here, either. Will's brother did too."

Leo cocks an eyebrow. "Ahhh, Will. Same guy you turned your cell phone down for, huh? Are you two in *loooooove*?" He draws the word out like he's a kindergartner.

Before I can reach over and slap him, he laughs. "Just kidding. I get it. You're a book nerd. He's a book nerd. It's a match made in heaven."

Actually, it would be a match made in a bookstore, but whatever. Will is just a friend. A friend who happens to read for fun, work in the bookstore I love, and binge chocolate turtles. Hopefully I can find a spot with a decent signal later so I can text Erica and tell her about him. She'd love that.

"Anyway, Will's brother saw something here in the ballroom a long time ago. Something that scared him really bad. I'm going to find more evidence, then see if he'll share his story with Mom and Dad. Between what I saw, what he saw, and my research, we should be outta here in no time."

"You think that will work?" He sounds eager.

"It has to," I answer grimly. "I can't stay here anymore. It's too scary."

I half expect Leo to make fun of me for being afraid, but he doesn't. Instead, he stands up, walks to the door, and looks out around the corner. "There's a lot of rooms here. Why don't you sleep in a different one from now on?"

"I might." I follow him to the hall and look at the row of doors. There's definitely plenty of other options. Since the eerie things have only been happening in my room, maybe...

Wait.

Why is that? Yeah, the light bulbs in the kitchen aren't easy to explain, but they still could be something with the wires like Mom suggested. But the creepiness in my room, that's a whole different story.

My blood runs cold. Could it be possible that the things happening in my bedroom are happening because of me? Are the Shadow People after me, specifically?

"I...um, I'm gonna go." I stumble out of Leo's room, my mind reeling. If I'm right, then getting Mom and Dad to believe in the Shadow People is even more important than I thought.

CHAPTER TWENTY-ONE

I decide not to sleep in a different room after all. Truth is, I am scared of the room I chose. But leaving it would be the biggest chicken move of all time. Agatha and Hercule Poirot would laugh in my face over something like that, and I wouldn't blame them.

Instead, I settle for waiting until everyone else is asleep and dragging my bedding to the hallway *outside* my room. I figure that's only half chicken because I can still see and hear everything going on inside, but there's no chance I'll get locked in again.

I miss you too! I reread Erica's last text message. She sent a picture of herself at Starbucks, holding our favorite drink—a chai latte with sweet vanilla cream. I turn away from the photo, frowning. She looks happy. A good best friend would be glad, but instead my stomach is tied into a painful knot. I text her back a simple heart emoji, then slump against the wall, trying to get comfortable on the hard, wooden floor. It's dark too. Even with my phone flashlight permanently on, there are shadows on top of shadows. Everything looks like a place for a monster to be lurking, and I hate it. Plus, with no electrical outlets close by, leaving my flashlight on means my phone battery will eventually die. Not good.

You awake? I text Will. It doesn't go through. I try again, then again. On the fourth attempt, it finally shows my message is delivered.

Yeah. Can't sleep.

Me either, I say back. I'm in a hot hallway trying to sleep on a wooden floor.

His response is slow this time, probably because I only have one bar on my phone.

???

I laugh. It seems like the kind of text Erica would send me. Just don't like my room.

I don't blame you, is all he says back.

What time do you want to meet tmrw? I ask. Again, the text takes forever to go through. Will probably thinks I'm the slowest texter in the world.

Wanna just talk when we wake up?

Sure, I say. A grin stretches across my face despite my crummy circumstances. The idea of Will researching with me is awesome. Tomorrow will only be my third day at Woodmoor, and I'm already exhausted. I don't want to do this alone anymore. I'm not even sure I can. The one thing I'm sure of is that I'll never survive a full month in this house.

Tomorrow, my plan is simple.

1. Test the skeleton key on any random doors
2. Open any drawer that isn't locked and go through the contents
3. Ask Will if Craig will talk to me about what he saw

It's that last part of the plan that worries me the most. If Craig won't even talk to his own brother, then why would he talk to me? I try to come up with arguing points in my head. I can help Craig finally solve the mystery of what he saw. That's good for him, right? Unless he doesn't care anymore. Or maybe he's embarrassed about it and knowing he didn't imagine it would make him feel better.

I don't know. All I can do is try. I curl up on my blanket and turn my phone light off. The darkness gobbles up the hallway, leaving me to stare at nothing. I close my eyes for a moment, then open them immediately. Is the clock louder all of a sudden?

Sitting up, I peer into my room. I can't see the mannequin, but I can see the fireplace and the door to the sunroom.
Everything looks fine. But it doesn't sound fine. The clock
has been ticking softly ever since we arrived, but at some
point, I must've learned to tune it out because it hasn't made
me as crazy today. Now it's louder, like someone turned the
volume up.

I stand up and let the blanket fall from my body. Just like
before, the ticking isn't coming from one direction. It's everywhere. In the floor, the walls, the ceiling. It's in the air.

It reminds me of Erica's house. Her parents got this fancy
stereo system put in about a year ago. There are speakers in
every room and one volume knob controls them all. They
can play the same music throughout the entire house, which
is cool. Well, except for the times they pick old music, which
is pretty often. It should be illegal for people to blare a song
called "Mr. Roboto" in every room of their house.

Tiptoeing down the hallway, I keep my phone flashlight
steadily shining into the darkness. When I reach the end, at
the stairwell that would take me up to the ballroom, I stop
and listen. The ticking grows louder. I take a few steps up and
pause again. Louder still.

I hate the idea of going up there, but I can't ignore this.
Proof doesn't just fall into Agatha's characters' laps, and it won't

fall into mine, either. I have to be willing to look for it—even in dark, scary ballrooms.

I take another shaky step up, somehow managing to put one foot in front of the other until I'm at the top. Standing at the mouth of the moonlit ballroom, I realize something: The clock doesn't sound like a clock anymore. It sounds like music, like a faint song hidden behind the sound. The ticking slowly fades away until all that's left is a melody. A scary one. I close my eyes and listen hard. The tune is hard to catch, but I manage to start a voice memo on my phone and hum a few bars.

When I look up from my phone, I have to clamp a hand over my mouth to keep from screaming.

The shadows. They're *everywhere*.

I stagger backward, crashing into the wall. I want to run, but I feel stuck. Attached to the floor just like the mannequin in my room. Instead, I stare in horror, realizing that unlike the shadow I saw in my room, these shadows have a shape. A very *human* shape. They move from one side of the room to the other, then abruptly stop as if I've interrupted them. In a flash, they turn toward me.

I gasp. The faces are *horrible*. Nothing but yawning black holes. But the eyes... The eyes are blood red. A hiss pierces the silence.

Like soldiers called to action, the shadows rush at me.

Their horrible red eyes begin closing in from every direction. The hissing gets louder and louder until it's almost deafening. Choking back a sob, I spin around to run, but the door is closed. And just like back in my room, the knob won't turn.

I'm trapped.

"No, no, no!" I cry out, pressing harder against the wall. A sharp pain catches me in the shoulder. The light switch! Turning around, I flip it on.

The shadows vanish. The room is empty and quiet. Blinking away tears, I slide down the wall and land on the floor. Someone, or *something*, wanted me to hear that song. They wanted me to hear it so badly that they lured me up here. Now I just have to figure out why.

CHAPTER TWENTY-TWO

Something hard nudges me in the side. I swat at it and roll over, groaning when it happens again. Cracking my eyes open just a slit, I see Leo hovering over me.

"What are you doing out here? Did you seriously sleep on the floor all night?"

I sit bolt upright. "What time is it?"

"Six thirty. Mom and Dad aren't up yet. I woke up because I had to go—"

"Yeah, yeah," I say, stopping him before he starts talking about the bathroom. I swear, teenage boys like to talk about that more than anything else. "Don't you have a bathroom in your room?"

He nods. "Mm-hmm. But now I'm hungry."

Of course he is. I look down at my phone, groaning when

I realize it's dead. No wonder my alarm didn't go off at six o'clock. I wanted to wake up before Mom and Dad, so I didn't have to answer any questions about sleeping in the hallway. Thank goodness for Leo and his weak bladder.

I quickly stand and gather my bedding. Then I take it into my room and dump it on the bed. I'll deal with that later. Plugging my phone in, I wait for the little battery icon to go away so I can get into my phone. I'm dying to start researching the song I heard last night—if the internet will let me, anyway. Even now it's already fading from my memory, so I'm glad I thought to record myself.

Closing my eyes again, I listen for the ticking. I stand like that for what feels like an eternity before I give up. It's gone. For the first time since we arrived at Woodmoor, the ticking is gone.

I slump against the wall, worry taking over. If the ticking is really gone for good, that means it only stuck around long enough for me to hear the song.

And those shadows. Ho-ly cow. I guess Craig isn't the only true witness anymore. I'm one too. But I can't be the one to tell my parents about this. Not if I want them to believe me. And I really, *really* need them to believe someone. This isn't just about getting back for the writing workshop. This is dangerous. Scary. We have to get out of Woodmoor.

When my phone is finally charged enough to use, I crouch on the floor so it can stay plugged in and play back the voice memo. The audio isn't great, but I can hear the few notes I hummed last night clear enough. Again, they send a wave of shivers up and down my spine.

The tune isn't familiar, but it's oddly powerful. It's also important. Now I just need to figure out why.

Walking over to my window, I look out at the fountain. The storms from yesterday have passed through, leaving behind blue sky and puffy white clouds. They look out of place above the dark tree line, the tree line where the Hitchhikers supposedly hide. When I first came to Michigan, I thought the Hitchhikers were going to be the scariest, worst part of my summer. Now I'd give anything to be dealing with a legend like that one. A monster that stays *outside* of the house. But no. The halls of Woodmoor are crawling with sinister things. So is my bedroom.

An invisible clock that plays music.

A mannequin that comes to life.

Shadows that turn the air icy.

It's time to get solving this mystery before something really bad happens.

The sound of a door in the hallway grabs my attention. I peek out just in time to see Dad shuffle out of his room and down the stairs. He's wearing a dazed morning look, the same one he always has before he's had any coffee. Still, he looks rested. Happy. That means whatever, or whoever, is bothering me is leaving him alone. I haven't had a normal night in Woodmoor yet, but Dad, Mom, and Leo seem comfortable. Why?

My phone dings. It's Will.

You need to come to the bookstore. Now.

I stare at the text, confused. It's barely past seven in the morning. Why is he at the bookstore instead of asleep like a normal teenager?

Why?

There's a long pause. One minute. Two. Three full minutes pass before a text dings.

I'll explain when you get here. Can you get a ride?

I'll try, I respond. Then I quickly snatch up some clothes from a pile on my floor, sniff to make sure they aren't disgusting, and put them on. Dad's meetings are today, so if I hurry, maybe I can get a ride into town with him. Racing down the stairs, I stop at the kitchen door. Dad is standing by the table in the middle of the room, his hands on his hips.

"Dad?" I say, immediately noticing the shards of glass covering the room. They're scatted across the countertops, the stove, and the floor. "What happened?"

Dad spins around, his face twisted in confusion. "I don't know. I replaced the bulbs that broke last night, but now they're *all* broken."

He carefully maneuvers around the bits of glass to the corner where Mom stashed the broom last night. "I'm going to tell the manager of the property she's got to get an electrician out here ASAP. This isn't safe."

No, it isn't, I think as I look up at the broken bulbs. There are three different light fixtures in this room. One above the sink, one in the middle of the room, and one around the corner in what Mom calls the "butler's pantry." Every light bulb in all three of those fixtures is shattered. I know Dad thinks it has to be an electrical problem, but I don't.

"I'll help you clean up," I offer.

Dad smiles, but it's half-hearted. "Thanks, kiddo. That would be great. I have to be in town for my first meeting in an hour and a half."

"No problem." I grab the dustpan and hold it while he starts sweeping in the glass. "Are you nervous? About the meeting, I mean?"

"A little," he answers. "There are a lot of people who don't exactly love Woodmoor Manor. It's going to be hard to change their minds, and I really need the help of the historical society to do it."

Poor Dad. He hardly ever sounds nervous. Not like this, anyway.

"You'll do a great job. You always do," I tell him, hoping he realizes I'm being honest. I might not like all of the old places Dad fixes up, but I have to admit they look pretty amazing when he's done. Still doesn't make me feel any different about staying at Woodmoor, but whatever. "Would it be okay if I ride with you? I mean, I won't go to your meeting. I want to go to the bookstore for a while."

"I suppose that would be okay. Scoping out the books or the boy?" Dad asks, his mouth curled into a teasing smile.

"Neither!" I roll my eyes at him. Dads can be the worst sometimes. "A friend wants me to meet him there."

"So, the boy."

When I don't answer, he starts laughing. "Joking! Your mother told me yesterday that when you came back to the car, you were with someone."

"Will," I say. "He works at the bookstore."

"Ahhh," he says, taking the dustpan from my hands. "Another bookworm. Maybe he could find out if the owner is hiring anyone else."

"Maybe." I gently use a napkin to start sweeping the glass on the table into a pile. "Will wants to work at a publishing company someday."

Dad nods appreciatively. "Perfect. The two of you could take over the shelves!"

"We'll probably never see each other again. After I leave here, I mean." It doesn't make sense, but the thought makes me sad. I don't even really know Will. I just know that he's kind and, for whatever reason, willing to help me.

"Don't count on it." Dad holds a trash bag just under the edge of the table so I can sweep in the pile of glass. "Friends are forever." He ties up the bag and gives me a squeeze. I lean into it, feeling grateful. Even when things seem bad, Dad has a way of staying positive. Upbeat. I love that about him.

"How about I go get dressed so we can get out of here? We could even make a quick stop at the bakery on the way into town and get you a cinnamon roll for breakfast."

My ears perk up. Will said to hurry, but my stomach is saying *feed me*. "That would be great."

He winks and heads back upstairs with two mugs of coffee. Mom is lucky. She didn't have to clean up *and* gets coffee in bed. I pull out my phone and text Will. Be there soon.

Then I park myself by the front door and wait for Dad. Whatever Will texted me for seems like a big deal. I just hope it isn't bad too.

CHAPTER TWENTY-THREE

I pull a wad of napkins from the paper bag. I got more frosting on my face than in my mouth, and I don't really want to show up at the bookstore like this. Using the little flip-up mirror, I scrub at my cheeks until they're clean. They're also red. *Awesome.*

Dad pulls into a parking spot. "My meetings will probably be a few hours at least. I'm afraid you're stuck here until I'm done. Is that okay?"

A few hours? I really should have thought this through. I want to find out what Will texted me about, but I also want to do some sleuthing back at Woodmoor. Solving mysteries would be a lot easier if I could drive a car.

"Um, yeah. I guess so. Just call me when you're done."

"And your ringer volume will be on?" Dad asks pointedly.

I sigh and nod. "If something happens and you can't reach me today, it's not because my volume is turned down. It's because the cell reception here is terrible. So annoying."

"It should be better here in town."

"That's what Mom said," I tell him.

"Well, she's right. Woodmoor is really remote, and since it's surrounded by a state park and the lake, there's no close cell towers. I'm not surprised at the lack of signal there. Anyway, have fun this morning, and I love you."

"Love you too." I open the car door and hop out. Even though the sign on the door says Closed, I can see Will waving to me from inside. I walk up and wait for him to unlock it, then step in.

"Why were you here so early?" I ask.

"Lilian is supposed to be working with this other guy, James, but he got a flat tire on the way here, so she called me. I don't have to be here all day. Just until James can get here."

"Oh," I look around. It's still dark in the store. Dark, but peaceful. Totally different from the darkness inside Woodmoor. I'm dying to tell Will about what happened to me last night in the ballroom, but the expression on his face stops me. He looks freaked out. "So, the store isn't open yet?"

"No. Opens at nine so we have to hurry." His voice is strained. "Come with me."

We head back to the same room we were in before. The room the typewriter is in. It's sitting in the same spot. Will points at it, his eyes stormy.

"What?" I ask. It looks the same to me. Same polished metal, same perfect keys.

He bends down and points at the paper. The word on the paper is different.

OUT.

At first, I don't understand why this is such a big deal. Greta must have figured out how to get the typewriter to work. The word on the paper yesterday was *get*. Now, it's *out*. I stare at the black letters, realization slowly dawning on me. When you put the two words together, it doesn't seem like part of someone's grocery list anymore. It seems like a message. A warning.

GET OUT.

Suddenly, the goose bumps are back.

"Did you do this?" I ask. "Because if you did, it isn't funny."

Will looks offended. "You're the one who told me this typewriter doesn't work, remember? How would I have done this?"

141

I start to answer him, but he continues.

"And why? To be a jerk? If I wanted to be a jerk, I wouldn't have told you all that stuff about me and my brother and..." He swallows hard. "Woodmoor."

Shame settles over me. He's right. Will has been nothing but nice to me. No way would he play a trick like this. "I'm sorry. I'm just a little scared is all."

"Me too," he says. "Because there's more. I talked to Greta about the typewriter this morning. When I said I was coming in to cover for James. She didn't know anything about it."

"What do you mean?"

"I mean that it just showed up here. No note, no explanation, nothing."

I lower down into a chair. An idea is coming together in my head and it's not good. My stomach churns and bubbles with anxiety. I'm scared. Really, *really* scared. But showing it right now would be the worst thing I could do. If Will knows I'm scared, he might get scared and decide not to help me. He might even decide not to hang out with me at all anymore. No, I have to stay calm. Stay focused. Get the job done and get out of here.

What would Agatha do? I think. She's the queen of mystery. Her characters are always in over their heads because she puts them there. The successful characters ask a lot of questions. Will and I need to ask a lot of questions.

"We should talk to the owner of the antique shop," I say, jumping up. "That's where my brother first saw the typewriter."

"When was that?" Will asks.

"Saturday. It was around lunchtime when we got here." I think back to that first drive down this little street. How I'd been pleasantly surprised that it wasn't grim looking, like Woodmoor. Little did I know something like this would happen—a mysterious typewriter with an even more mysterious message. "Maybe this is all just a coincidence. There's no proof that those words have anything to do with me. Right?"

No one ever talks about the town being haunted. Only Woodmoor and its woods. Yet now this mysterious message is showing up in town, right when I've shown up in town. Even though I would like to think it is, it doesn't seem coincidental.

"I don't think it's a coincidence," Will says, shaking his head gravely.

I point at the word typed on the paper in stark black ink. "So, you think this message was meant for me?"

Will meets my eyes. "I do."

That makes two of us. "I have a theory. I can't prove it yet, but I will."

"You gonna share it with me or make me guess, Sherlock?"

"Haha," I say sarcastically. "I'll share but don't laugh. I think the Shadow People are much more than just a legend."

Scratch that. I *know* the Shadow People are more than just a legend. I learned that the hard way. "Maybe they live in Woodmoor and don't like visitors. That's why there are so many scary stories about them. What if they act up because they don't like it when people are in the house?"

"Yes! And your family is living there," Will adds, excitement in his voice. "So, the Shadow People are super annoyed."

"Exactly. I just can't figure out exactly why they're mainly targeting me. Unless they know I don't want to be here anyway, so they think they can get rid of me more easily than the rest of my family."

I look down at the typewriter, pressing a few keys on it for the second time. Again, the little metal piece doesn't leave a mark. "If that theory is true, then the typewriter makes sense too. I mean, what better way to try to reach *me* than through a typewriter?"

I expect Will to comment on my idea, instead he asks, "Soooo, you don't want to be here?"

There's a glimmer of something in his expression. Disappointment, maybe?

"Oh. It's not that, really. It's just that it's not exactly a retreat, you know? The house is kinda scary. Plus, I'm missing something to be here." I look down at my sneakers, suddenly embarrassed. What I want to tell Will is that so far, he's the only good thing here in Michigan, but that would be weird. Instead, I decide to change the subject. "Hey, if Greta doesn't know why the typewriter is here, do you think we can take it with us?"

"Do you *want* to take it with us? Because I'm thinking about smashing it, to be honest," Will answers, a weak laugh giving away his nervousness. It's kinda nice to know I'm not the only one afraid right now.

"I know. I don't like this either. But if there's a chance this thing is sending me messages from...someone—" I pause; we both know that when I say *someone,* I mean the Shadow People. "—then I need to have it with me. I could see the messages faster."

Will's head slowly nods. "I'll leave a note for Greta that I'm figuring out why it showed up here. That's partly true. We'll take it with us and go to the antique shop."

"Smart. Maybe they can tell us where they got it to begin with."

"You think that could be a clue to who wrote the message?"

I shrug. "Dunno. Agatha puts a lot of things in her books that *might* be clues but also might be something called red herrings. A red herring is a fake clue."

His eyes light up. "Oh, you mean something to throw the reader off, so they don't figure out the mystery too fast."

"Exactly! I think this typewriter is too much of a coincidence not to be related to the spooky things happening at Woodmoor, but we'll see."

Pulling his phone from his pocket, Will groans. "It's almost nine thirty. Store will be opening any minute, and I'll have to go out front."

Just then, an older, taller boy walks into the back room. He's got sleepy eyes and very ruffled hair. He looks from me to Will then back to me again. "Hi?"

He asks like it's a question. I give him an awkward wave.

"James, this is Ginny. She's...ahhh, in town for a while."

James smiles and tips his chin upward. "Hey. Where you from?"

"Chicago," I answer.

"Nice to meet you, Chicago," he says, shrugging a backpack from his shoulders and tucking it into a corner. "You guys can go do whatever it is seventh graders do on a Monday in a boring town."

"Eighth," I say at the exact same time as Will. We look at each other, then laugh. I figured we are about the same age based on when he said he started coming here, but now I know for sure.

Will and I smile at each other. Then he lifts the typewriter with a loud groan.

"Heavy?" I ask.

"Crazy heavy."

"We can take turns carrying it." I hold the door open for him and then follow him out. Time to get to the antique shop and get some answers.

CHAPTER TWENTY-FOUR

"What do you mean you've never seen it?" Will asks incredulously. The typewriter is sitting on the counter in front of us, surrounded by piles of random things. Old key chains, rusted bottle openers, a license plate... This shop sells some weird stuff.

The woman behind the counter shakes her head. She pushes her glasses up her nose and bends down to inspect the typewriter one more time. "I'm sorry, Will, but I mean I've actually never seen it. It's a truly lovely piece, but it didn't come from my shop."

My jaw drops. It's not possible. Leo saw the typewriter in the window just three days ago. "My brother... He thought he saw this typewriter in your window on Saturday. Is there any chance you might have someone else working here who put it there and didn't tell you?"

She refocuses on me. Pulling the glasses from her

face, she nestles them into a mound of salt-and-pepper hair on top of her head. Poor lady has the same hair I do. Fifty percent wavy, fifty percent curly, and one hundred percent annoying.

"I'm sorry, dear, but that isn't possible. My husband, Arthur, and I are the only ones who work here. We don't bring in new items without discussing them first." She takes another glance at the typewriter, then looks back to me. "Plus, I was here Saturday. All day. Even if Art *had* purchased something for the store without telling me, I would have noticed it."

"Okay. Thank you, Mrs. Sheldon." Will heaves the typewriter up off the counter and heads for the door, me on his heels.

"Oh, Will?" she calls from the counter. "The typewriter is beautiful. Once you figure out who the owner is, send them my way?"

"Sure," he says, then under his breath, "Unless I smash it to bits first."

I open the door for Will, then gently close it once we're outside. "Want me to take it now?"

I try to sound brave even though I'm not. I don't want to touch that thing. Sad, because I've always wanted a typewriter exactly like it. Just, not one that's possessed and sending creepy messages.

"Nah. You carried it the second half of the way here. It's my turn."

We walk about a half block before seeing a bench. Will grimaces as he sets the typewriter down on it. "We can't just wander around with this thing. We need a plan."

Rummaging in my bag, I pull out my notebook. Good news for Will is that I always have a plan. I make a few notes, flip it closed, and turn to face him. "As soon as my Dad can drive us back to Woodmoor, we'll go with him and take the typewriter with us."

"When do you think that will be?"

I check out the time on my phone. "Probably about an hour and a half still. Maybe longer."

"An hour and a half of carrying this thing around?" He shoots a dirty look at the typewriter. "That sucks."

It does suck. Especially since I have no idea what we'll do to kill the time. Unless...

"Hey, is the ice-cream shop open yet?"

"It opens at eleven. Why?"

I could lie and tell him I only want to go there because I want more chocolate, but I'd feel bad. Plus, something tells me Will would know that's not true. "Just listen to everything I have to say before you answer, okay?"

"Oookay. I get the feeling I'm not going to like what's coming."

"Maybe not, but if you hear me out, I think you'll agree." I take a deep breath and tell myself to get it over with. Like ripping off a Band-Aid. "I want to talk to Craig. Ask him a few questions. I know you said he doesn't talk about it, and maybe he still won't, but if he finds out something in Woodmoor is terrorizing me, he might change his mind."

"I don't know, Ginny. He gets really upset if I bring it up. He doesn't even know you."

"I get that. I do. But something happened to me last night. Something worse than the mannequin."

"And you're just now telling me this?"

"I'm sorry. I didn't bring it up because we were so focused on the typewriter that there just wasn't a good time. I saw the shadows, Will. They were all over the ballroom. I can't tell my parents yet, though. Not without another witness."

"And you want my brother to be the other witness?" he asks.

"Yeah. Think about it—if something bad happened to you and then you found out it was happening to someone else and you might be able to stop it, wouldn't you want to?"

He thinks on this for a minute, then nods. "I guess so. Just don't blame me if he shuts us down."

"I won't. Promise." I open my notebook again and show him the page. "This is where I'm keeping track of all the clues so far. See this one?" I tap on the page where the words *ticking song* are circled. "This is important."

"Ticking song," he repeats. "What does that mean?"

A warm breeze blows my hair into my eyes. I brush it away. "There's been this ticking sound ever since we arrived at Woodmoor. Like a clock. Only it wasn't a clock. Not one I could find, anyway. And then last night it got louder. That's why I went up to the ballroom. It led me up there."

Will's eyebrows pinch together. "I'm confused. Your clue says *ticking song*, not just ticking."

"Right! Last night, it wasn't just ticking. There was a song behind it." The memory makes me feel jittery all over again. Like I'm back in that dim ballroom, listening to that ghostly melody.

Will's eyes widen. "What song?"

"I don't know. I've never heard it before. I listened long enough to memorize a few bars and hum it."

I open the voice memo and play it for Will. Somehow, even with the sun shining and the street beginning to fill up with travelers, it's just as eerie as it was last night.

"I don't like this, Ginny." Will looks from my phone to me. "I don't know why you're so calm about this, but this is really messed up. We're in over our heads. We need help."

Oh no. Will cannot start pushing to tell someone about this. I'm not ready yet.

I wave my hand in the air like his idea is silly even though it isn't. Under any other circumstances, I would agree with him. All of this is bad. Really bad. But I still don't have any concrete proof of it. Without that, I'm stuck here.

"It's fine."

"It's *not* fine," he argues. "Look, most people would be peeing their pants over the shadows and the song and the typewriter and...all of this! But you seem, I don't know, *excited*. Why? Is it just because you like mystery novels? Because this isn't fiction, Ginny. I think we're in danger. I think *you're* in danger."

"I know it's not fiction," I snap. "I'm scared every time I'm in Woodmoor! But I have to stay calm, or I'll never see this through. Plus, the thing I said I'm missing back home is a writing workshop. I really wanted to go to it, but Dad got this job and made us all leave. If I can prove to my parents that Woodmoor is a dangerous place, then I might be able to get out of here *and* back home in time for the workshop."

"They won't believe you if you just tell them?" he poses.

"Would you?"

His silence is my answer. Who *would* believe a story like this? It sounds like one of Agatha's novels. "I need proof before I tell them about this, Will. Solid proof. Without that, it will seem like I'm making up things so they take me back home."

"You have proof, though," he argues. "You saw the shadows yourself!"

I nod sadly. "Yeah, but I *might* have cried wolf a few times in the past. If I tell my parents about the shadows, they'll think it's just another *burying a body in the backyard* story."

"A what?" Will asks, laughing.

"Never mind. Let's just say that I've told them some things in the past that didn't end up being exactly true. They won't believe me about this. I promise."

Will's expression is unreadable. He stays quiet for a few long moments before finally saying, "Then I'll help you. I'll help you talk to my brother."

"Really?"

"Really."

I can't help it; I throw my arms around him. "Thank you!"

He laughs and hugs me back. "What, did you think I was going to ditch you?"

I pull away and give him a half shrug. "Kinda. You scared me with all that *we're in danger* stuff."

"I still believe that, for the record. I think we need to be really careful here. How much time do we have? I mean, if we are going to get you back home for the writing thing."

"It starts on Wednesday," I say glumly. "My best friend Erica is signed up too, and she's going to be in it alone. The whole thing just sucks." I choke back the tears I can feel building. No. I will not cry. That would be even more embarrassing than admitting that I kinda-sorta like Will.

Will picks up the typewriter and balances it against his chest. "Then let's go talk to Craig right now. We've only got two days to convince your parents to send you back home, so we can't waste any time."

CHAPTER TWENTY-FIVE

Will stops outside the ice-cream shop. He sets the typewriter on the ground, panting. "Let me handle this, okay?"

I quirk my head at him. Will has been trying to talk to his brother about this for years. I don't know why he thinks this time would be any different. "Okay. Why?"

"I have an angle."

"An angle?" I ask, snorting. "Now who sounds like the mystery writer?"

He swipes sweat off his forehead and flicks it at me. I dodge it, then take two steps back to be safe. What is it with teenage boys?

"I'm serious, Ginny. Just let me try, and if that doesn't work, then you can chime in. Deal?"

"He's *your* brother," I answer. Still. I hope I get a chance to do at least a little talking. "Hey, where's the other paper that was in this typewriter? The one with the word *get* on it?" My brain is still stuck on the proof thing. Even though I'd have to do some explaining, if I had both pieces of paper to show my parents, it would at least back up my story.

Will bends down and wiggles the edge of the paper that's sticking out of the machine. "This is it. At least I think it is. I never touched the other paper."

I stare at it, bewildered. So, the typewriter that can't actually type sent us a mystery message that vanished and a new one replaced it? I'm not sure even Agatha would come up with something that unbelievable.

"You ready?"

I bend down and lift the typewriter. Will tries to take it from my hands. "I got it. You go find Craig. I'll wait at a table."

He taps on the door and waits for someone to open it. Smirking, he says, "You'll actually wait? Because waiting doesn't really seem like a strength of yours."

"Shut up, Will."

An older man with a friendly smile opens the door. "Heya, Will! How's it going today?"

"Great, Mr. Ferguson. I'm just here to see Craig for a minute. Is he here?"

"Yup. He's in the back room going through some new

stock. Chocolate-dipped waffle cones!" He waggles his eyebrows and I laugh. "Anyway, you just go on back there."

"Thanks," Will says with a wave. "This is my friend, Ginny. She's just going to wait for me if that's okay."

"Fine by me. Nice to meet you, Miss Ginny."

I smile and follow Will in, shivering as the air conditioning inside the ice-cream shop hits my skin. I hadn't noticed how much it has warmed up outside. I bet Woodmoor is going to feel like the inside of an oven later. A ghostly oven.

I set the typewriter down, caught on that last idea. Ghostly. I've never really thought about what the Shadow People are, actually. Are they monsters? Ghosts? Spirits? Are ghosts and spirits the same thing?

Whatever they are, they're jerks.

Just as I'm lowering down into a chair, Will shows up. Craig is beside him. I notice that the smile I saw on his face yesterday is gone. He looks wary.

"Um, Ginny this is my brother, Craig. Craig, Ginny."

Craig lifts his head in a small nod and sits down. "I asked to take a break since we haven't even opened yet, but I only have a couple minutes. So, what's up?"

I look at Will. He mashes his lips together tightly. His hands are clenched into a knot on top of the table. He's nervous.

"Ginny's dad got a job here for the summer. It's at Woodmoor."

Craig flinches.

"Anyway, they're staying there, and some *things* have started happening to Ginny. Bad things. We were hoping you would tell us what you saw there. When we were kids."

Craig stands up to leave, but Will grabs his arm. "*Please.* Just this one time. I know whatever you saw that day scared you, but we need your help. Ginny needs your help. The thing in Woodmoor is after her."

"I don't know how telling you what I saw is going to help." Craig's blue eyes land on me. I think he's waiting for an answer.

"You're proof that I'm not imagining things," I tell him. "You're the only proof, actually."

"I'm not proof of anything," he scoffs. "I was a little kid. Back then I wanted to be a superhero when I grew up. Probably just made up some dumb new villain that day." He looks down at the table and runs a finger over a small heart and set of initials carved into the top.

"I don't believe that." I glance at Will to make sure I'm not talking too much. He nods for me to keep going. "I think you saw something scary and it's easier to pretend you didn't because it doesn't make sense. I get it. I'm scared too."

Silence settles over the table. I'm expecting Craig to stand up and walk away for good any minute. He doesn't.

"What do you want to know?"

I pull out my notebook and pen. "Everything you remember. No detail is too small."

He pulls the *Eat More Chocolate* hat from his head and runs a hand through his hair, just like Will does. "I was upstairs in the ballroom playing catch with Will. The ball went into a corner. It had some boxes and stuff in it. There were some tables too. I walked over to the corner to pick up the football and that's when I saw it."

I swallow hard. "Saw what?"

"The woman," he whispers. "At least I think it was a woman. It was a dark figure with long hair and glowing eyes. Bright red glowing eyes." Craig shudders.

I try not to show how freaked out I am, but it's hard. A shadowy figure with glowing red eyes? Sounds almost exactly like what I saw last night.

"Did she do anything?" Will asks. "Like lunge at you or whatever?"

"No. She said something, though."

I lean in, shaken.

Will's face is bloodless. His blue eyes are stark against his pale skin. He opens his mouth, then snaps it shut again. I know what he wants to ask...what we need to ask. I'm just not sure we're ready to hear the answer.

"What...what did she say?" I ask, my voice trembling.

Craig looks at me so closely I can see my own reflection in his eyes. *"Get. Out."*

CHAPTER TWENTY-SIX

"Are you okay?" Craig asks. He reaches out and jostles my shoulder.

"Yeah. I'm just...processing, I guess."

My heart feels like it's in my throat. Will and I suspected that the message on the typewriter could be connected to Woodmoor, but we didn't know for sure. Now we do. I thought I'd feel better, like we're making progress, but instead I feel scared.

"Now you see why I never want to talk about it." Craig slides the hat back onto his head. He swivels in his chair to look at Will. "I'm sorry, dude."

"For what?"

"For leaving you behind." He gives a sad shake of his head. "I didn't avoid talking about it all this time just because it was scary. I avoided it because I'm embarrassed. I was so afraid that day I couldn't even think straight. A good big brother wouldn't have left you behind."

"Like you said, you were a little kid. I don't blame you for running away. I mean, I would have done the same thing," Will offers. His voice is gentle.

Craig looks up. "You would have?"

"Totally," Will says. I don't know if he's saying this because it's true or he's just trying to make his brother feel better, but it doesn't matter because Craig is smiling now. A real smile too. Not just a smile that says he's relieved to be done talking to us.

Slapping his hands on the tops of his legs, Craig stands up. "I should get back to work, but Ginny?"

"Yeah?"

"Be careful. The rumors are true; Woodmoor is a bad place." He looks at Will, then back to me. "You two are messing with something dangerous. Something dark."

The tone of his voice makes me want to pack my bags and start walking back to Chicago. Up until last night, everything I'd done was to get back home for the writing workshop. That's still important to me and all, but now there's so much more at stake.

This is all playing out *exactly* how Agatha would have wanted it to. I'm trapped somewhere dangerous, like the Orient

Express in a snowstorm. Bad things are happening. A deadline is looming. I tell myself once this is all over, I'm going to stick to writing mystery novels rather than living them because this is awful.

"I know. I'm trying to get away from there. If I need you to, would you be willing to tell my parents what you just told us? About what you saw?"

"If it means getting you out of Woodmoor, sure." Craig squeezes Will's shoulder, then walks back behind the counter.

Will turns to face me. "All these years I thought he was embarrassed that I saw him get scared."

"He's a good brother."

"Yeah," he says wistfully, watching Craig load fresh drums of ice cream into the freezers. "Now what? We got his story. We also know that the typewriter message is linked to Woodmoor."

What *is* next? I feel like I just bought a ten-thousand-piece puzzle and dumped the whole thing out on the floor. We have a lot of clues, but no idea how they all fit together.

"Can you still come back to the house with me?"

"Probably." Fishing his phone from his pocket, Will sighs loudly. "Or not. Just got a text from my dad. He needs help getting the boat back in the water today. We had to pull it out last week for some engine repairs."

"You guys have a boat?" I blurt out.

He waves a hand dismissively in the air. "Don't get excited. It's small and mainly for fishing. Not some big fancy thing you can grill out on or anything."

Still. A boat sounds fun. I mean, for someone who isn't battling Shadow People in her spare time.

"I'm sorry. I gotta go. My dad is outside." He stands, then does a double take as if just remembering the typewriter. "Wait, can you carry that?"

"I carried it before," I say, lifting it as proof. Holy cow. It *is* heavy. Now I remember how hard I was huffing and puffing by the time we got to the antique shop. I was determined not to let Will notice so he didn't try to carry it again. I pull a smile onto my face even though the metal is biting into my fingers. "I'm good."

He looks skeptical but nods. I follow him out and find a bench to sit on, typewriter at my side. Will gives a quick wave and hops into a car idling at the curb. I've never seen his father up close, but I can imagine what he looks like. Friendly smile, blue eyes, and graying hair. Like an older version of Craig and Will. I bet he's nice, even if he is obsessed with schedules and boat maintenance on vacation.

I pull my phone out and text Dad. How much longer?

I'm on my way, he replies. Meetings went well!

Well that's good, I guess. Dad has worked hard to build

a reputation for his business. A long time ago he hardly had any clients. Then he got some bigger projects and did good work, so word spread. I've heard him talking and know how important it is that his clients are happy when he's done. I'm sure that's extra important here since this is his first big job outside of Illinois.

Okay. I'm by the ice-cream shop.

I tilt my face up toward the sun, enjoying the heat on my cheeks. Sad to think that in a short half hour, I'll be back at Woodmoor. Dark, ugly Woodmoor. Dad sure has his work cut out for him.

I guess I do too.

CHAPTER TWENTY-SEVEN

Once Dad finally stopped asking me questions about the typewriter sitting in the trunk of the car, he started talking about his meetings. I'm grateful. His questions were tricky to answer, and I don't like to lie. In the end, I told him that the bookstore is letting me borrow the typewriter for a while to see how I like it. Not a total lie.

"So, the good news is everyone likes the ideas so far," Dad says in a chipper voice. I realize I zoned out and must've missed something.

"Oh, um, that's awesome!"

"Definitely. I'll spend the next few weeks researching and working with the historical society, then I'll put together a proposal for what they need to renovate at Woodmoor so they can host events. If they take my suggestions, it will cost them a lot, but the manor should start making money in no time."

I smile enthusiastically. I'm glad he's happy right now, especially since he'll be very *un*happy once I can prove to him that we need to leave.

"What's the bad news?" I ask.

He turns away from the road just long enough to give me a quizzical look. "What bad news?"

"You said, 'the good news is,' which usually means there's bad news too." Agatha Christie books haven't just taught me how to solve mysteries. They've taught me to listen carefully. Paying attention to what people say, or don't say, can make a big difference.

Dad chuckles. "Nothing gets by you, does it Ginny?"

I smile.

"There isn't any bad news. Not really. It's just that people in this area have opinions about Woodmoor, and opinions can be hard to change. That's all."

"They'll change their minds when it's done." I try to stay positive, but the seed of a bad idea has lodged itself in my mind. I shove it out, refocusing on my phone when it dings in my lap.

Sorry I had to bail.

It's a text from Will. I tell him it's no big deal even though it is. Now I'm going to have to do all the sleuthing by myself this afternoon. I don't know if Leo will be home, and even if he is, I don't think he'd be a big help. Skeleton keys and mystery doors just aren't his thing.

My phone dings again. I thought of something. When you show your parents the evidence, do you think they will just move you guys into a hotel?

His text is like a bucket of ice water dumped over my head. I hadn't thought of that. I figured Dad would move into a hotel while he keeps working here and Mom would take Leo and me back home. But would my parents be so desperate to keep our family together that they'd move us *all* into a hotel? I consider it, eventually deciding it isn't likely. A hotel for over three weeks in a town this nice would be expensive. We would need at least two rooms every night for the four of us too. That would add up. Fast. We're not poor, but we aren't rich, either. Plus, a lot of the places here aren't even hotels; they're inns, which cost more, I think.

No way, I text back. $$$

I get back an emoji that looks like it's sweating with the word Good.

Looking up from my phone, I notice that we're on the last stretch of road leading up to the manor. Dread coils in my stomach. I hate this place. Hate the road, the trees, the stupid parking lot, and the creepy NO CAMPING sign.

Most of all I hate the house.

"Shall we?" Dad asks, putting the car in park. He hops out, whistling cheerfully as he walks toward the front door. I mumble a yes and haul the typewriter out of the trunk. Slowly. The paper hanging out flutters in the breeze. Between this machine typing out warnings, the Shadow People, and the mannequin moving around at night, I have no idea how I'll ever sleep in Woodmoor again.

Dad unlocks the front door and lets me walk through first.

Mom walks out of the kitchen. Her cheeks are bright pink, and her mouth is set in a hard line.

"You okay?" I ask, setting the typewriter down on the table.

"Just realized I don't have some of the ingredients I need to make dinner."

Poor Mom. Her cooking experiences never go the way she wants them to.

"Let's just order a pizza," Dad suggests.

Mom swipes the back of her arm across her damp forehead. The kitchen must be brutally hot. "I don't know if any restaurants will deliver all the way out here, but we can try."

Dad kisses her on the forehead. "I'll call around. You relax."

Mom gives a tired shake of her head. "Well, I'm not going to argue with that. The heat in here is getting to me a little today. Thank you."

Dad heads upstairs. Mom plops down in a dining room chair, eyebrows pinching together as she catches sight of the typewriter. "Ginny! Did you buy this? How? Where?"

I laugh and hold my hands up. "Don't get excited. It's not mine." *Thank goodness.* "The bookstore owns it. They're letting me borrow it to see how I like it. You know, to decide if I want to invest in one of my own."

"Well, that's nice of them. I take it your friend had something to do with this?" She arches an eyebrow, clearly hoping I'll share something about Will. Not gonna happen. Mom's love that kind of gossip. I don't really mind her thinking I might like Will, but I don't want her telling everyone else about him. Especially since I'll never see him again after this summer, anyway.

"Kinda," I murmur. Lifting the typewriter, I tip my head toward the stairwell. "I should probably get this upstairs in a safe spot. Don't want anything to happen to it."

I pause in the doorway. "Did Dad tell you about the light bulbs? They were broken again when we got up."

Mom stands and pushes the chair in. "He did! I changed the bulbs again and just left the lights off for now. At least there's a window in there and the sun has been out today. The electrician is supposed to come out tomorrow to take a look."

He won't find anything, I think. I know it's a message from the Shadow People. *Get out. Leave or we'll make your lives miserable.*

I make it to the stairwell before I give up and set the typewriter on the ground. I need to write some things down before I forget them. Actually, I need to *draw* some things before I forget them. Sometimes a list just isn't good enough.

Pulling out my notebook, I turn to a fresh page and write Rooms Where Creepy Stuff Happened. Then I draw a sloppy sketch of Woodmoor's floor plan. It's nothing but a rectangle split into small uneven squares.

The main floor includes the entryway, a guest bedroom, a living room, a library, dining room, kitchen, butler's pantry, and eating area. The second floor includes all the bedrooms, a dressing room, some storage spaces, and an office. The third floor is the ballroom. I label each space, then make a star in each room where something strange has happened. Kitchen: broken bulbs. *Star.* My bedroom: moving mannequin, whispers, cold air, shadows. *Star.* Ballroom: shadows, ticking song. *Star.*

Now that I look at the activity mapped out this way, I realize that even though a lot of the strange things have happened in my room, the rest of the house hasn't exactly been peaceful. In fact, there's been some unexplained happening on all three floors.

Strange. I look from one square to the next. Bedroom, kitchen, ballroom. One room on each floor. But why those three rooms? Could there be a connection between them?

I put my notebook away and heave the typewriter back up off the floor. Time to get to work. The stairwell is sweltering hot, but at least it's well-lit. For now. I need to get as much research done as I can while the sun is up because once it goes down and the house grows dim again, I'll be too afraid to investigate.

CHAPTER TWENTY-EIGHT

Erica's face is stony as she listens to my story. I know I need to be productive while the sun is up and the house is bright, but I'm feeling sorta...homesick. I miss Chicago, and Erica, and everything summer should've been. Just one phone call won't take up too much time.

"So, you're telling me you're living in a haunted house?" she asks.

"I don't know if haunted is the right word exactly, but yeah. Bad things are happening here. I need to get home, Erica."

Her eyes soften. "Bad things? Not to sound like a jerk or anything, Gin, but do you think maybe you're just letting one of your dad's dumb old buildings get to you?" She pauses like she's remembering something. "Like that hotel! What was it called?"

"The Oaks. And no. That was different." I think back on

the times I visited The Oaks with Dad. It was old and needed repairs, but I never saw anything scary there. No shadows, no whispers, no mysteriously locked doors. Just a bunch of peeling wallpaper and musty, cobwebby corners.

Erica's face freezes for a few long moments before going back to normal. Stupid reception in this place. It's impossible to use the internet for more than a minute at a time before losing connection, and phone calls aren't much better.

"Can you hear me now?" she asks, but her voice is broken up and robotic.

"Yeah." I lower my voice so I can't be overheard from the hallway. "I'm seeing and hearing things here. I'm not the only one, either."

Erica looks horrified. "Not gonna lie, this sounds like the plot to a horror film. What did your parents say? They have to be scared too, right?"

"No. They haven't said anything because they don't exactly know about it yet."

Her face scrunches up into a mess of confused lines, then my screen glitches and it's back to normal. "They don't know? How is that possible?"

"They haven't seen all the stuff I have. The only thing that has happened around them is some breaking light bulbs, and they believe that was the electricity."

"But you don't?" she asks.

"I know it wasn't," I say grimly.

Our connection lags again. I sigh and wait for it to clear up, hoping this isn't the time it quits working for good.

"Hey, is that Leo?" Erica asks, narrowing her eyes on the screen. She starts waving.

"What?"

"Behind you."

I whirl around, my heart picking up speed. There's no one there. "You... You saw something just now?"

Erica nods. "I thought I did. Must have just been the glitchy screen. Looked like a person standing behind you. Figured it was probably Leo spying on our call."

A chill washes over my clammy sweat-soaked skin. I take another glance at the space behind me. It still looks empty. But is it? I breathe deeply, the bad feeling I have most of the time here in Woodmoor growing stronger.

"Ginny? You okay?"

"Yeah," I answer, a nervous hitch in my voice. "I meant to say I'm sorry I haven't called or texted. For one, we're in the middle of nowhere and my phone doesn't work very well. For another, I'm *trying* to get out of here and home. Maybe even by Wednesday."

Erica's eyes light up. For the first time, I notice she's

outside on her rooftop deck. Erica lives in a condominium. All the owners get to use the rooftop deck, which is amazing in the summertime. You can see Navy Pier, the skyline, the whole city really. A pang of jealousy hits me. Why can't I be there with her, sipping lemonade in the sun while she sings completely off-tune?

Soon, I remind myself. I just gotta stay focused. Hercule Poirot never gives up on a mystery. He investigates and interviews until he has the whole thing sorted out. If I want to be able to write that kind of character someday, I need to learn the ropes. Do my own research. I need to be dedicated, no matter how horrible things get. Plus, if I give up now, I'm stuck here for the whole month.

"Wait, you're trying to get home by Wednesday? Do you think you might make it back for the workshop?"

"Working on it," I say with a weak smile. "But that's only forty-eight hours from now. It's gonna be tough."

Erica smiles into the camera. "*You're* tough, Gin. You can do it."

I smile back. I hadn't realized I needed to hear that, but I guess I did. I feel better now, less overwhelmed. "Thanks. Oh, I do have some help here. His name is Will. He works at the bookstore and is helping me gather proof of what's happening in Woodmoor to show my parents."

"Will, huh? What does Will look like?"

"Light brown hair, blue eyes, a few freckles... Why do you want to know?"

She giggles. "Just want a visual of your vacation boyfriend."

"Will is *not* my vacation boyfriend. He's just a friend."

Erica laughs harder. "Riiiight. 'Just a friend.' You should hear yourself! Plus, you're totally blushing."

Am I? I swivel around to look at myself in the mirror on the dressing table and scream. Instead of my red cheeks, I see ghostly white skin. And eyes. Red eyes, exactly where my own eyes should be. A mouth filled with broken teeth sits just below them, hung open in a scream.

I stumble backward and trip over the chair, crashing to the ground. My phone flies out of my hand and slides across the floor. Crawling across the rug, I snatch up the phone and slowly turn back toward the mirror. The face is gone.

"Gin? Ginny!" Erica is screaming. Her voice is chopped up into mechanical sounding bits and pieces of words.

Turning the phone back around so I can see her, I finally give in to the fear clawing around inside me. The tears I've been holding back run down my cheeks in fat streams, quickly soaking the collar of my shirt. Her face is frozen, but I don't care. I need to talk to someone about all this.

"Did... Did you see that?" I ask, hiccups breaking into my words.

Her image unfreezes. "See what? What happened?"

I sniff and swipe at the tears. "I saw a face. In the mirror. I was looking to see if my cheeks were actually red or if you were teasing me, and it was just...there. It sort of looked like a woman." I let my eyes flutter closed and think about the face. Porcelain white. Red eyes. Mouth open in a scream. What *was* that? No... *Who* was that?

"Call the police. Call them now."

I shake my head bitterly. "And tell them what? That I'm seeing faces and shadows in here? Everyone in this town already thinks Woodmoor is cursed. They'd probably just ignore me."

Someone yells in the background. Probably Erica's mom. I look back at the screen and notice that at some point, Erica went back into the house. Her face is as white as a sheet.

"I gotta go, Gin. But please...promise me you'll get help with this."

"I will," I tell her, but I can tell she doesn't believe it from the way she's shaking her head. "I mean it."

I *am* going to get help. Will's help. Then I'm going to show Mom and Dad exactly what they're dealing with here and get out...just like the Shadow People want.

CHAPTER TWENTY-NINE

I feel light-headed now. Sick, too. I head into the bathroom and fill the sink with water. With shaking hands, I splash it onto my face. I thought my room was safe during the day. Up until now, it seems like most of the bad stuff has happened at night when it's dark. Not anymore. Apparently, now there is no safe time.

You're okay. You're okay. You're okay. I keep repeating it to myself even though I don't believe it. I can't stop thinking about the face in the mirror. Erica was right; this *is* like a horror movie. And unfortunately, right now I'm the star.

Pulling a towel down from the rack, I dry my cheeks and neck. I look back up slowly, half afraid there might be something scary in this mirror now too. There isn't. Just the same cloudy mirror. Except...

I blink at the reflection of the room in the background. I've never really looked at it from this angle. I spin around. Standing here, I can see that one side of the curtain is not cinched and tied up like the other side. The fabric is hanging loose and billowing gently. My window is open. Only a crack, but still. I didn't open it. I stare at the fluttering curtain, fear crashing over me in waves.

"Get it together, Ginny," I hiss at myself. I can investigate this. I need to investigate this. I'll never get back home to Erica and that lemonade if I don't.

My legs tremble as I creep closer to the corner. Seriously, there are so many windows in here—why does the one with the wonky curtain have to be by the mannequin? Talk about rotten luck.

Even with the figure's head covered, it's still eerie. I try to keep my distance and close the window at the same time but can't. I either need to suck it up and get closer or find something long I can use to push the window back down. Where did Dad put that umbrella? I know it's a display item, but using it just one time to close a window shouldn't damage it. I look under the bed and in the sunroom before giving up. No umbrella. I'll have to use my arm.

Goodbye, arm.

I tentatively reach past the mannequin's head and place

my palm on the bottom of the window. Then I shove down until it's firmly closed. The curtain falls flat. I gather the folds of fabric in my hand. Cinching them together, I shakily re-tie the little flap so that it stays gathered.

That's when I spot the holes. Four of them, just level with the mannequin's head. They're small and blend into the flowery wallpaper. Probably why I never saw them before. Plus, I've tried *really* hard to avoid this corner.

Tracing the space between the holes, I notice that if you connected them, the shape would be a rectangle. Something was hanging on this wall before. A picture? I snag my notebook and jot down the words holes—important? Maybe this isn't a clue to anything, but I can't risk ignoring it.

"Everything okay?"

I yelp and press a palm to my chest. "Mom! Don't sneak up on me like that!"

Mom is standing in the doorway. "I didn't mean to startle you. I just came up to see how you are and...well, you look a little...stressed?"

I bet I do. My face is still damp, my hair is sticking to my sweaty forehead, and my heart is about to beat out of my chest. Not my finest moment. "I'm okay. Just noticed my window was open. Did you open it?"

She nods. "It was just so stuffy in here. This room was

built to allow more sunlight in than the rest of the house, so it naturally heats up."

Ah. No wonder this room always feels like a furnace. "Why? I mean, do you know why it was built that way?"

Mom makes a humming sound. She's thinking. "I actually don't think I ever heard why, specifically. Maybe Dad could find out for you if you need to know?"

I shake my head. This room is hot, but I need to stay focused on the things that matter. The real clues. Otherwise, I'll get distracted and never figure out what's happening in Woodmoor.

"Okay, then. If you're all good, I'm going to get showered up. We finally found a restaurant that will deliver pizza here. Should be here in about an hour. Sound good?"

"All right." I force a smile to my face. Nothing sounds good right now. I'm juggling too many clues and don't have any that make sense. How will I write books like Agatha did if I can't even solve one measly mystery of my own? I bet she'd have all these clues put together and everything solved by now. She'd have proof and might even be on her way back to Chicago. I mean, if she lived in Chicago.

Mom vanishes back into the hall. I move the tipped-over chair back into the sunroom where it originally was and then pull my suitcase out from the corner. The skeleton key is still tucked deep in the pocket where I hid it. I pull it out and turn it over in my hand, looking for any markings that might be a clue. There's nothing. Just smooth silver metal. I should've told Will about this. I would have if I hadn't gotten so caught up in the typewriter, and Craig, that it slipped my mind.

I snap a picture of it and send it to Will. Ever hear of a secret door in Woodmoor?

A response comes faster than usual this time. No. Do you think there is one?

Maybe. Found this in a pile of normal keys.

What is that? Will asks.

A skeleton key. I don't think they're used anymore so this has to open something interesting.

The dots show up on the screen again. Will is typing. It stops then starts up one more time before revealing his message. Be careful.

Oh, I'll be careful all right. I just saw two red eyes and a scary mouth in my bedroom mirror. Even Agatha's characters wouldn't be brave around something like that.

CHAPTER THIRTY

An hour later and I've gotten nowhere. I've searched every inch of every bedroom on the second floor. I've found a lot of dust bunnies, a handful of spare change, and a used Q-tip (gross), but no secret door.

I quickly slip out of my parent's room and into the hall before anyone catches me. Explaining why I'm creeping around in there wouldn't be easy since it's one of the most boring rooms in the house. A bed, a window, a dresser, and an old machine. Actually, I think it's a type of record player. I've seen them in pictures before.

Leaning against the wall, I fan my face. It's so hot in here. Every room I walk into is more stifling than the last. Maybe I should stop for a while. Take a break. Finding a secret door doesn't guarantee that whatever is inside of it will help me piece together these clues, anyway.

Although, the key has to unlock *something*, right?

I decide to check one more spot. Opening a storage closet, I scan the shelves. There are stacks of clean bedsheets, some towels, and a couple of WET FLOOR signs tipped over on the ground. I push them around to make sure nothing is hidden behind them, then sigh. Nada. Zilch. *Nothing.*

I slam the closet door, then open it and slam it again. It feels good to let myself be angry, just for a minute.

"Dude. Why do I always find you in this hallway freaking out?" Leo suddenly appears. He has a slice of pizza in one hand, and a Coke in the other. "You're like Hank."

My mouth flops open. Hank is our neighbor's dog. He's a tiny little fluff ball of a thing that pants and shakes nonstop. He's literally the most nervous dog I've ever met. I'm *nothing* like Hank. I'm calm. Collected. I'm a future bestselling novelist researching for her future bestselling novel!

"I'm not freaking out," I argue. My voice wobbles a little. I stand up straighter to be more convincing. "And I'm not like Hank. I'm just looking around is all."

"Looking around, huh? For what? The ticking again?"

Why are brothers so nosy? "None of your business!"

Leo frowns. "It's totally my business! You're snooping around because of what you told me before. *The Shadow People.*" He looks up and down the hall warily, then refocuses on me.

"Did something else happen? Because I deserve to know these things too. I'm staying in the same house as you, you know."

"Yeah, but they aren't bothering you." I slide down the wall until my butt hits the floor. Then I slump over and groan. "Typewriter messages, mystery song, skeleton key, face in the mirror, holes in the wall..."

"What are you talking about?" Leo interrupts, lowering to the floor beside me. Pizza crumbs cover the front of his shirt and pants. "Seriously. You're making no sense. I know you saw a shadow in your room, but typewriter messages? Mystery songs? What does that even mean?"

"I can't tell you what they mean because I don't know yet! I'm trying to put all of the clues together and find proof—*real proof*—that we need to leave, but I'm failing." I hold out my hand and show him the skeleton key.

Leo takes the key and turns it over, inspecting it. "Is this real?"

"It's pretty heavy to be fake, but I don't know for sure. It was in that basket of keys I threw at you in the kitchen." I take the key back and stuff it into my pocket. "Maybe it doesn't open anything, but I gotta at least try. I have too many clues right now, and no matter how I look at them, they don't fit."

"Still don't understand how this place can be haunted if I've never seen or heard anything."

Haunted. There's that word again. It sticks in my brain, reminding me of the bumper sticker I saw that first day we arrived at Woodmoor. *Warning, this vehicle makes sudden stops at haunted houses.* Maybe that was a clue. Right now, I don't even understand what or who the Shadow People are. They *could* be ghosts. I know they want us to leave, but why? What's so special about Woodmoor that they keep chasing everyone away?

"I believe you and all, it's just weird." Leo opens the same closet I just searched. When he's convinced there's nothing interesting inside, he shuts it again. "You never answered me, by the way. Last time you were this upset, you mentioned hearing a clock. Do you still hear it?"

"No. Last night I was listening to it carefully and something happened. It turned into a song." I leave out the part about the shadows in the ballroom. I don't want to scare him. Leo wouldn't be my first pick for a sleuthing sidekick, but he's better than no one. Searching this place alone, especially once the sun starts setting, wouldn't be fun.

My brother tilts his head to the side. "A song?"

I shrug. "Yeah. It's hard to explain, but the song seemed... I don't know...hidden in the ticking? Once I heard the tune, the ticking went away."

"Mmmkay. I never heard the clock or the song, so I can't

really help there, but I guess I could look around with you. If you want me to."

I snort. "*You* want to help me search the house?"

Shrugging, he looks up and down the hallway. "Why not? I want to go home too. Plus, it's not that *scary* in here."

"Okay, then." I don't know what else to say. Leo offering to help is...different. Like, I wouldn't say we're usually enemies or anything, but he's not exactly helpful most of the time. Unless helpful means loud and messy, then he's got things covered.

"So, tonight?" He stuffs the last bite of pizza into his mouth, then washes it down with a long swig of Coke. "Maybe midnight?"

"Midnight? Why would we search the house then?"

Leo looks at me like I'm speaking gibberish. "Um, maybe because everything creepy happens late at night? If you want real proof, then you need to search the house when there's the highest chance of scary stuff happening." He stands up and wipes the crumbs from his pants. "Oh, we need to video it too. I do that with most of my games back home so I can put together clips of all my good ones."

My mouth flops open. What is happening? Is Leo *actually* making good suggestions?

"Midnight it is," I tell him, then stand up. "And make sure your phone is charged so we can use the flashlight!"

We'll need all the light we can get.

CHAPTER THIRTY-ONE

Maybe there's a mystery door in the ballroom.

I'm standing in the quiet hallway, waiting for Leo to come out of his room when the idea hits me. I don't like it. My last experience in the ballroom was scary, and after hearing Craig's story, I'm even more frightened to go up there again. Plus, I'm still feeling shaky from seeing the face in the mirror. I've tried to sketch a picture of what it looked like in my notepad, but it's hard. The features weren't clear. More than anything they were just pieces of a woman's face and a ghostly shade of white laid over my own reflection.

Leo's door opens a crack. He peeks out, only opening it all the way when he sees me. "Ready?"

I'd say yes, but I'm too busy laughing. Thick black bands hold a GoPro on Leo's forehead. The red light is already flashing. He looks supremely dorky.

"Ha-ha," he whispers, adjusting the small camera so that it's straighter on his head. "Thanks to my brilliance, you'll have your proof by the end of the night!"

I sure hope so. I made a list of all the clues I have so far before meeting Leo. It's overwhelming. I don't even know what's important and what isn't, so I decide to do what Hercule Poirot does and trust my instincts. If I *think* something is important, I'm keeping it. That leaves me with a long and mega-confusing list.

Clues:
- Shadows in my room and ballroom.
- Song behind the ticking.
- Typewriter message.
- Skeleton key.
- Holes in my wall.
- Bulbs in kitchen.
- Connection between kitchen, ballroom, and my bedroom?

"Where are we starting?" Leo whispers.

"Ballroom," I answer through gritted teeth. I don't want to do this. Not even a little.

Leo nods and steps back so I can lead the way. I turn on my phone flashlight and tiptoe down the hall. The floor creaks under my feet. I stop a few times, praying that Mom and Dad don't hear us and come out. I have no clue how we'd explain Leo and his nerdy GoPro.

When we finally reach the end of the hallway, I pause at the base of the steps. They're dark. Pitch-black, actually. Even with my phone light it's going to be hard to see.

Leo nudges me from behind. "What are you waiting for?"

When I don't answer, he nudges me again. "Gin?"

"I'm scared," I admit. I didn't mean to say it. The words just slipped out. I look down, embarrassed.

"It's okay. I am too."

I turn back to face him. Even though I wish he wasn't recording this moment, I'm glad Leo is here. "You are?"

He nods and tips my phone down, so the light isn't shining in his eyes. "Who wouldn't be? It's a big, creepy house that's apparently filled with monsters or ghosts or whatever."

I nod and try to get back some of my courage. It's hard when I know what's waiting for me. For *us*.

"Want me to go first?" he offers.

"No. I'm good." I take a shaky step up, but Leo tugs on my shirt sleeve.

"You can ask for help and still fix the problem, you know. Agatha Christie probably had a bunch of people helping her. No way she wrote all those books alone."

No, she didn't write all those books alone. Agatha had a whole team of people at her publisher helping her. I didn't expect Leo to know that, though. In fact, I didn't really even expect him to remember her name. Maybe he pays more attention than I thought.

I shoulder into him with a laugh. He's on the step below me, which means I accidentally bump into the camera. "Thanks, dork."

"Ow," he says, straightening the GoPro again. "You're welcome. Violent, but welcome."

Turning back around, I take a deep, calming breath and start walking. One step at a time. I try not to think about what's waiting for us at the top. Instead, I focus on the sound of my own breathing and the idea that by tomorrow morning, all of this will be over. I'll be showing Leo's video to Mom and Dad. Maybe it won't even matter if I can put all the clues together. As long as they see something scary on this video, they'll let us go home.

When I reach the top of the steps, I slide over so Leo can follow me into the room. We shine our phone lights around the cavernous space. It's empty. Quiet, too. Maybe too quiet. I shine my light directly into the center of the room and motion for Leo to do the same thing. Then we start walking. *Together.* Flashes of moonlight dot the wood floor. Wind rattles the old wooden windowpanes. The darkness surrounding us feels terrifying. Alive. I have the feeling that we aren't alone.

We reach the middle and stop. Leo's phone light jumps around in the darkness. I glance at him, confirming my suspicion. His hand is shaking. Bad.

"I don't see anything," he breathes.

"I don't, either."

Just then, a sound echoes through the room. It's distant, but familiar. Leo looks at me, eyes wide. "What is that?"

Click.

Click.

Two more times, then silence. The wind picks up, making a groaning sound against the windows. My heart is racing, and my legs feel like overcooked spaghetti noodles. *I know that sound.*

"Oh my god. It's the typewriter."

CHAPTER THIRTY-TWO

Leo follows me downstairs, his palm trembling against my shoulder the entire way. The typewriter clicks several more times, then stops. We stop too.

"They heard us," Leo whispers. His strained voice sounds scary in the otherwise quiet hallway.

"They?"

He nods, the movement barely visible through the darkness. "Yeah. I think whoever was typing heard us coming."

My entire body tenses with the thought. Is someone or something in my room right now? I tilt my phone flashlight in to brighten the space. It flickers over the weary flowered wallpaper and small crystals hanging from the chandelier.

"Just turn on the light," Leo says.

I nervously reach my arm around the corner and sweep

my hand over the wall until I feel the light switch. When I flip it upward, nothing happens. "Won't turn on."

A hiss of frustration escapes my brother. Or maybe it's fear. Either way, I can see lines of worry on his face through the darkness, and they make me feel even worse. Leo isn't the worrying type. If anything, he's more of the *act now and think about it later* type. I'm glad I'm not alone right now, but I hate that I dragged him into this.

"Where's the typewriter?" Leo asks.

"It's in the sunroom. That little room to the left after you walk in." I point my phone in that direction, freezing when a creak breaks the silence.

"What was that?" Leo asks.

Taking a step back, I shake my head. "It could be the mannequin again!"

"It could also be the wind," Leo argues.

Old places like this do make a lot of odd noises. But Leo could just as easily be wrong. I squeeze my eyes shut, trying not to imagine the mannequin moving across my room. Maybe it's right inside the door and I can't see it. Maybe it's waiting for us...

I spin around, fully prepared to run. I'm not embarrassed about being a chicken this time. Maybe I was wrong about experiencing a mystery so I can write them. I don't want to experience it anymore.

My brother grasps me by the elbow. "Don't, Ginny. Don't run from it this time. Maybe whatever—or *whoever*—is doing this keeps it up because you let it."

I tug my elbow out of his grip. "Yeah, well, we're going to need to find a different way to deal with this because I can't do it anymore. I'm too scared, Leo. You haven't seen the stuff I have." I sniff angrily. "Every day it's something new. Something worse."

"I get it," he says quietly. "But you're not alone this time. I'm here, and I'm sick of this dumb *whatever it is* messing with you."

A little piece of me is grateful to hear that. Most of the time I don't think Leo would throw a bucket of water on me if I were on fire. But right now, in this dark hallway with who knows what prowling around my bedroom, I think he actually cares.

Taking a long, deep breath, I refocus on his face. It looks determined. "Okay, but if we die, I'm blaming you."

We creep across the threshold. I stop just inside the door, hold my breath, and quickly shine my phone light toward the mannequin. It's in the corner where it belongs. The mirror looks normal too. Still, I wish the lights would turn on. Being in the dark makes it hard to think...to *breathe*, even.

"I don't see anything," Leo whispers, swiping the sweat from his forehead. He angles his phone toward the fireplace, then around the edges of the room until the light lands on my rumpled bedding. "Except proof that you're a slob."

I make a face at him that he probably can't even see. "Look who's talking Mr. *Use too much body spray instead of showering!*"

My brother snorts in response. "Whatever. You're just as gross as I am. You just don't like to admit it."

He's not entirely wrong. I've only taken one real shower since we got here. The other times I just cleaned with soap and a washcloth. Unlike Leo, though, it's not because I'm lazy or just don't care if I stink up everything around me. It's because the running water is too loud. The mannequin could sneak up on me, and I wouldn't even hear it.

I can just see the headline: MYSTERIOUS SHOWER ATTACK LEAVES ONE DEAD.

No thank you.

We make our way into the sunroom where the typewriter is sitting on the small table in the corner. I hesitantly approach it, then stop in my tracks. Even through the dim lighting, fresh ink is visible on the paper. When I finally gather the courage to take the last few steps toward it, I'm winded by what I see. New words.

CHAPTER THIRTY-THREE

poorhomeallbent

Before I can even think about what the new message means, a crash breaks the silence. I scream. Leo runs to my door, stubbing his toe on something in the darkness along the way.

"Ow, ow, ow." He's jumping on one foot now, hobbling further into the hall. I follow him, my heart hammering against my ribcage.

Mom and Dad's door flies open. Mom emerges first, then Dad. I shine my phone light toward them, tipping it down when they shield their faces from the brightness.

"What was that? Did you two hear something?" Dad shouts, jogging toward the stairwell that leads downstairs.

I swallow through the thickness in my throat. Of course

we heard it. If I didn't know what kind of house we're staying in, I'd think a plane crashed into the roof.

"I'm going to check downstairs." Dad takes a few steps in that direction but stops when I call his name.

"The ballroom," I say. "I think it came from the ballroom."

Just then the hallway lights flip on. Leo startles so hard he loses his one-legged balance and topples to the floor. Mom rushes away from the light switch to help him up.

"You go ahead and check downstairs. I'll go look around upstairs in case Ginny is right."

Dad's face wrinkles up like it does when he's concerned. "I don't think that's a good idea, honey."

Mom laughs. "It's fine. We're not dealing with the boogeyman, here."

Riiiiiight.

"We'll go with her," Leo offers. "Do you think you'll be okay downstairs? Alone?"

Wordlessly, Dad marches back into their room and comes back out with the same heavy silver candlestick he had a few nights ago. "I held the record for most home runs in Little League when I was eight. I think I got this."

I laugh. None of this is funny, but seeing my parents trying to be brave even when they're scared is hilarious. It's just one more thing about being an adult I'm not looking forward to. If I have kids someday and they tell me there's a monster under their bed or in their closet, we'll probably just have to move.

Dad chuckles and heads downstairs. I grab my notebook and follow Leo and Mom down the hall.

"You two don't have to come up with me, you know," Mom says, pausing at the base of the steps. "I promise I'm not afraid of a few bumps in the night."

Leo slides the camera back onto his head and straightens it the best he can. The red light is flashing again. "I'm not either."

Mom looks bewildered. "Are you filming? For heaven's sake, Leo, I'm in my pajamas!"

"It's a good idea," I tell her. "If there's damage up there, won't you guys need to be able to show the owner people what happened?" I hope Mom buys this excuse. Really, I just want another chance to capture something strange on Leo's camera.

"Exactly!" Leo says excitedly. "Don't want them to blame me and my basketball like that other hotel did."

I cross my arms over my chest and give him a dirty look. "Um, they were right to blame you. You *totally* broke that window!"

My brother opens his mouth to argue, but Mom shakes her head. "Enough, you two. Let's just go get this over with so we can all go back to bed."

Leo grumbles and turns on the light switch. The narrow space brightens. I can't help but notice how dark the ballroom looks at the top. Like a gaping black hole.

And we're walking straight into it. The hairs on the back of my neck rise. I loosen the fists my clammy hands are curled into and shake them out. I'm going to be okay. We're all going to be okay.

"You wanna follow her?" Leo whispers.

I shake my head and rub away the goose bumps on my arms. "You go next so you get a clear view. Make sure you video the whole room. There could be a clue we missed when we were up here before."

He nods and takes the stairs two at a time to catch up with Mom, who is already standing at the top.

When we reach her, the first thing I see is Mom's open mouth. Her jaw is dropped, her eyes wide as she focuses on something in the distance. I turn the lights on, the air hissing out of me when I see what she's staring at. One of the big windows set into the angled ceiling is broken and a tree limb is sitting on top of Mom's baking supplies. The boxes that hold her things are crushed. Bits of wood and leaves are scattered throughout the room.

"How...how in the world," Mom breathes, approaching the area slowly.

"Mom! Be careful!" Leo points at the shards of glass littering the floor.

Mom sidesteps them, crouching down next to the boxes. I do the same, wincing at the destruction. Wooden utensils are snapped in half, bowls are shattered. And Mom's precious mixer, the one I only recently wished she'd never bought to begin with, is mangled.

She picks through things carefully, eventually saying, "Well this is bad luck. Must've been a dead limb. Too bad it fell right over this window. Looks like most of my things are ruined."

"Most of them?" I croak out feebly. I feel terrible. Even though I don't love Mom's new cooking hobby, it makes her happy. The fact that the Shadow People just took that away from her is wrong. "I'm sorry."

I turn to look at Leo. His lips are downturned as he surveys the mess.

"It's okay. Nothing we could have done about it." She maneuvers around the glass to the broken window. A gentle breeze is wafting through it, filling the stale room with humid, sweet-smelling air. "I just can't believe this. If this limb had broken off the tree and fallen just a few feet that way," she gestures to the left. "It would have fallen on the roof and not the window."

"It's not that windy, either," Leo adds. "Wouldn't it have to be really bad weather to cause that?"

Not if this is connected to the typewriter message we just got, I think to myself.

Poorhomeallbent. I imagine spaces between the words, mouthing them slowly. *Poor home all bent.* The message plays on a loop in my mind. Even though it isn't as scary as the first one was, it's still bad. Especially since it showed up right before the limb crashed through the window.

I open my notebook and scribble down my thoughts before they get away.

- Poor home = Woodmoor?
- All bent = broken window?

Was this message another warning? If it was, then Mom's busted kitchen supplies could be payback because we haven't left Woodmoor yet or because we were prowling around in the ballroom when something—or *someone*—doesn't want us here. Nobody got hurt tonight, but that doesn't mean it won't happen eventually if we stay.

Mom shrugs. "Maybe, maybe not. The tree could be damaged or sick. This limb could have been ready to break at any time. But it does seem strange..." She trails off, the first sign that Mom might be getting suspicious about Woodmoor.

She should be. It's obviously not just out to get me, anymore.

It's after all of us.

CHAPTER THIRTY-FOUR

Back in my room, Leo rubs his eyes. He looks at the typewriter again and shakes his head. "This is the kind of stuff in movies, Gin. I can't believe that just happened. The message and then the tree limb." His voice wobbles, and I look away. I hate seeing my family like this—worried. I just don't know how to fix it yet.

"I know," I respond grimly. "Tonight changed everything."

"How do you mean?"

"Up until now, the…" I search for the right word. "*Spirits* or whatever haven't done anything dangerous. That tree limb was different, though. It destroyed all of Mom's stuff."

"True," Leo mumbles, glancing around my room nervously. The light switch worked this time, so we aren't in the dark. Still, something is off. The whole house feels like that, really, but especially my room. It reminds me of how the ticking sound was loudest in here. "We're lucky we weren't still up there when it happened."

I look away from the typewriter, horrified by the thought. Leo stood right in that spot just minutes before the limb came down. It would've smashed us flatter than a penny.

I quiver as I look from one window to the next, the skeleton-like trees rising up into the night sky just beyond them. "This." I point to the words the typewriter spit out tonight. "I think this was a threat. The Shadow People don't want us here. They tried to get us to leave by scaring me. Now they're targeting Mom. Eventually they'll do something to all of us."

"Don't they know we don't have a choice? I mean, seriously! I don't want to be here. There aren't even any televisions in this stupid place!" Leo raises his fist like he's going to bring it down on the table, but I reach out and stop him. I hold my finger up to my lips, reminding him we have to stay quiet. Mom and Dad spent forever covering the window upstairs with plastic. They just went back to bed, and I don't want to wake them up again.

"Mom and Dad won't ignore this. Tomorrow they'll call us downstairs and ask to have a family meeting like they always do. They'll say we're leaving. They have to."

The voice wobble gets worse. So does the ache in my

stomach. I wish I could agree with him. "I overheard Mom telling Dad it was just a fluke." I blink, my eyes burning with exhaustion. "She doesn't suspect something paranormal. Neither of them do."

Leo drops down onto the couch and groans. "So, what now? Because I'm not up for being terrorized all summer."

I sit down next to him, feeling rattled. I don't know what now. Tonight was supposed to be big. I was going to get proof that Mom and Dad couldn't ignore. Then I was going to pack my stuff so we could go home tomorrow. Now I have the exact same thing I've had since we stepped foot inside Woodmoor.

Nothing.

"I don't know." My lip trembles with the admission. "I thought we'd get something good on video tonight for sure—something Mom and Dad couldn't call a fluke, like the shadows in the ballroom, or the mannequin moving, or the face in the mirror."

"Wait," Leo says. "Shadows in the ballroom? You never told me about that."

"Yeah. I'm know. I just have so much going on that my brain is beginning to feel cramped." I look up at the ceiling, wishing I were looking up at my ceiling back home. I'm struggling with *everything*. I can't sleep, I can barely eat, and now thanks to this message I know I'm not being paranoid.

I'm in danger.

"I can't help you unless you tell me everything. There's obviously a lot I don't know."

He's right. There's a stage in every good mystery novel when the reader is dying to solve the case but can't. They're usually still missing an important clue, sometimes more than one. This is that stage for Leo. I've only told him a little of what I've shared with Will.

"I'm sorry. I should have been filling you in on this stuff, but I thought I could handle it myself. Plus, Will has been helping me."

Leo's eyebrow jumps up. I shove him playfully. "Knock it off. We're just friends. His brother saw something creepy in this house when they were little, and I think Will has been looking for answers ever since."

"Let's get them then. Maybe Will could come here tomorrow?" my brother asks hopefully. "Think about it. Mom might already be having second thoughts about staying here. The light bulb thing and now the tree limb. She could be easier to convince if we have solid proof, even if it's small. We could search the house together!"

"Yes!" I say, drawing out the *s* sound at the end with excitement.

Leo shuffles toward my door, the GoPro dangling from

his hand. He stops just before walking out. "You gonna be okay in here tonight?"

Glancing at the typewriter, then to the mannequin and the mirror, I shrug. "It might be another hallway night for me. I'm tired, but I don't think I can sleep in here."

"Sleep in my room," he offers. "I found a ton of extra blankets and stuff in the closet yesterday. You can use those to make a bed on the floor."

I tilt my head to the side, positive he's joking. "Um... Are you voluntarily being nice to me?"

He gives a half laugh. "Yeah. Don't worry, you still drive me crazy, but I'm not going to leave you in a haunted room. I'd feel guilty if the ghouls ate you overnight."

"Gee, thanks," I say sarcastically, snagging my pillow from the bed and my phone charger from the table before he changes his mind.

"No problem. Pay me back when you're a rich and famous author someday."

I smile at the idea. I don't even need to be rich and famous. I'd settle for the chance to be an author. Too bad I have to survive Woodmoor first.

CHAPTER THIRTY-FIVE

Dad's voice drifts up the stairs, waking me up.

"I'll get that limb situation dealt with as quickly as possible," Dad says. "I'm so sorry about your things, honey."

I crack an eye open and force myself to sit up. Pain shoots through my neck and back. Ugh. Sleeping on a hard floor is the worst.

"Not your fault," Mom says. "Like I told the kids, it was just bad luck. Other than a few minor setbacks, it seems like things are going well, no?"

A muffled yes filters through the door, then Mom's voice again. "Good. You've always wanted to expand the business. Get out of Chicago. This is your chance!"

"I hope so. I need this project to go well. Based on what the historical society has been telling me, it's going to be hard to get the folks in town excited about this place again. Sounds like most of them would rather see it torn down, to be honest."

It gets quiet suddenly, so quiet that I sneak over to Leo's door and press an ear to the wood to hear them better.

"Don't think about that. If anyone can turn this place around, it's you. It's beautiful, just needs a little TLC."

Dad sighs. It's just loud enough to send a pang of concern through me. "I hope you're right. No matter how good my plans are, this place is going to struggle without the support of the community."

"They'll support it. Just imagine how elegant Woodmoor will look when it reopens. Folks will be lined up to stay here," Mom murmurs. I squish my ear flatter against the door, so flat it hurts my cheekbone. "So, stop worrying. The meeting is going to be great and so will you."

I slowly pull away from the door, feeling dazed. Dad has another meeting today—a meeting he sounds worried about.

Suddenly I don't feel so good about my plan. Dad loves this project. He also believes it's going to help his company, which helps our family. He'll be *so* worried when I show him whatever evidence Leo, Will, and I dig up today. Plus, what will happen if he finishes this job and it doesn't help Woodmoor start making money? Because it might not. If the real problem isn't the yellowed wallpaper and ugly light fixtures, but the

Shadow People, then dad *can't* succeed. Right? He could change every single thing about this place from the floors to the ceilings and people still won't want to stay here. In fact, if they try to, the Shadow People will become even more dangerous.

Poor home, all bent.

I move back to my blankets on the floor, my stomach in knots. The situation seems more complicated than ever. Dad might stay here, alone, in this terrifying house. That's not safe. And once the job is done, Woodmoor will look nicer, but the problem will still be here. The Shadow People will just keep chasing people out one after another, just like they did to Craig...and me.

Dad will think he failed. His company will lose money, maybe clients. And my parents will be stressed.

My plan slowly begins to unravel right in front of my eyes. I can't go through with my original plan. Not without hurting Dad and his business, anyway. There has to be a different way, a way to end this rather than just escape it.

My heartbeat quickens in my chest. *End it.* Is that it? Instead of letting the Shadow People chase me away like everyone else, maybe I need to chase *them* away. Show them they don't belong in Woodmoor anymore. If I can do that, Dad has a chance at succeeding. And I'd still have a chance to get back home to enjoy at least a little of my summer before eighth grade rears its ugly head.

"You're scheming," Leo's groggy voice pipes up from beneath the covers. "I can tell by the way you mash up your face."

"Did you hear any of that?"

He pulls upright. His hair is sticking straight up, and there's a crease down the side of his face. Must be from the seam in his pillow. I try not to laugh and fail.

"Haha. Laugh at the tired guy," he says with a yawn. "And yeah, I heard some of it. Why?"

"Don't you see what this means? We can't just leave here, Leo. Not even if they tell us we can."

He suddenly looks much more alert. "I thought that was exactly what we're trying to do. Get out of here."

I stand up and start pacing. "We are, but not like this. I want to go home. *Bad.* But if we convince Mom and Dad that it isn't safe here, do you really think Dad will go home with us? Do you think he'll give up this job?"

I can tell Leo wants to say yes. Things would be a lot easier that way. Instead, he falls back against his pillow with a loud moan. "Why do you have to think so hard about everything, Ginny? Why? We had a plan!"

"A plan that wasn't fair to anyone but us!" I snap. Leo

turns over on his side and puts the pillow over his head. I march over and tug it off. "Hear me out. When we were going into my room last night, you told me to stop running from them. That maybe the Shadow People are terrorizing me because they know they can. Remember that?"

He tries to pull the pillow back, giving up when I shove it behind my back, out of reach. "Yes. So what?"

"You were right." The realization shocks me. Leo...right. And not just about something, about *everything*. "Everyone who comes to Woodmoor ends up running away. Will's brother, visitors...everyone. That's the problem. Woodmoor can't make money if the Shadow People stay here. It's up to us to get rid of them, or Dad will look like a failure."

Leo's eyes find mine. They're filled with concern. "You think so?"

"Yeah. Will you still help?"

Scrubbing his hands down his face, he nods. "I'm in."

A mixture of relief and sadness washes over me. I'm happy that Leo isn't backing out even though he knows what we're up against, but I'm sad because this is it. This is goodbye. Goodbye to my chance at a normal summer. Goodbye to the writing workshop. Goodbye to going home soon.

And then there's the biggest goodbye of all...goodbye to staying out of danger.

I bite down on the inside of my cheek to focus on something other than the tears stinging my eyelids. I don't have time to cry about this. Agatha wouldn't. She'd roll up her sleeves and get to work. It's time for me to do the same.

CHAPTER THIRTY-SIX

An hour later, Will is on the doorstep. He grins when I open it, the lopsided smile making me feel better immediately. "I brought stuff."

My eyes glide to the backpack he's hoisting off his shoulder. It looks heavy. "What kind of stuff?"

"Mostly books. My boss let me borrow anything I thought we might need, so I raided the local history section."

"You told her about this?"

He laughs and shakes his head. "Um, *no*. I told her I'm doing a project for a writing workshop."

The words send a pang of sadness through me. *The workshop*. I should be there tomorrow, sitting next to Erica and learning all the things I need to know about writing my first mystery novel. I should be drafting my first chapter of

The Shadows of Woodmoor and sharing it with Erica to see what she thinks. Now? I'm sweating and shaking and prepared for another day of misery. I don't even know if I'll ever be brave enough to write that book. Not after everything that's happened.

"There's still time," Will says softly, as if reading my mind.

I purse my lips together rather than tell him the truth, that I'm not going to try to get back for the workshop anymore. Even thinking it hurts. But there isn't a choice. Once I realized my family is in danger here, I had to put them first. I have to solve this mystery and send the ghosts packing for good.

Then I'll text Erica. She's gonna freak.

"Thanks for the books. The internet is so bad that computers and phones are kinda useless here."

"Yeah, I figured. Your texts take forever to come through." Will walks further into the foyer and peers around. "Wow. It looks exactly like I remember it."

"Haunted?" I ask, laughing nervously.

He chuckles. "I was going to say 'old,' but yeah, I guess 'haunted' works too."

"Dad is supposed to be fixing the old part, not that it matters." I wave a hand around the dim space, remembering the first time I saw it. The musty smell and the ticking had freaked me out immediately. I should have turned around and walked back out right then and there.

Mom rounds the corner and stops just short of Will, surprise written on her face. "Oh! I didn't know we had a guest. I'm Ginny's mother."

Will holds out his hand. "I'm Will. Nice to meet you."

My mother looks pleased. I'm not surprised. She already thinks I have a crush on him.

"We're gonna hang out with Leo around the house today. That okay?" I decide to change the topic before Mom says anything embarrassing.

"Of course! I'm headed into town to look for a new mixer, and your father has an important meeting here shortly, so just steer clear of that, okay?"

I nod, grateful that she isn't suspicious about Leo and me willingly spending time together.

"All right then, have fun. There's plenty of food in the fridge if you guys get hungry while I'm gone."

Slinging her purse over her shoulder, Mom rushes out the front door. I gesture for Will to follow me and head up the stairs. "I wasn't making up the part about my brother being here. I hope it's okay if he helps us?"

"Oh, for sure. The way I see it, you can use all the help you can get."

"What makes you say that? The mannequin roaming around my room," I grumble. "Or the fact that a tree limb smashed my Mom's stuff last night?"

He stops in the middle of the stairwell, eyes wide. "A tree limb smashed your Mom's things? How?"

"Yup. It flew through a window in the ballroom. That's why she's going to get a new mixer. The other one got crushed."

I shake off the thoughts, remembering we have a job to do today. *I* have a job to do today.

I'm already sweating when we reach the top of the stairs. Knocking on Leo's door, I brush my hair off the back of my sticky neck.

Leo opens the door right away. He reaches out and tugs me in, then Will.

"Get in fast. Dad was up here just a while ago asking what my plans are for today." He shuts the door behind us and throws himself on his messy bed.

"So? Mom knows Will is here. She said it was fine. Why would Dad care?"

"He's got some meeting. Said we can't get in the way or we'll need to go outside and 'explore the grounds.'"

There's not much I'd like to do less than explore the grounds. It doesn't matter how pretty they look, like everything

220

else here, they're probably dangerous. Plus, if Dad sends us outside, we won't be able to search the house.

"No problem," Will says. "My grandmother lived with us for a year before she went to a nursing home, and I had to be quiet because she slept like twenty hours a day."

Leo laughs then immediately apologizes. "Dude, I'm sorry. That isn't funny."

Will cracks a smile. "No, it kinda is. I tiptoed around for a year. Literally." The two of them laugh together. "And Grandma is fine. Just not at my house anymore."

"All right," Leo says, clapping his hands together. "Let's do this, then."

I pull my notebook from under my arm and set it down on the bed. "This is where I'm keeping clues." I flip a few pages in. "And here's a rough sketch of the rooms in the house. I propose we split up and search the house. Three floors, three people."

Leo scoffs. "No way. We aren't splitting up, Gin. That's a terrible idea."

I look to Will, but he just shrugs. "Will you be mad if I say I agree with him?"

Sighing, I rest my hands on my hips. "No, but this place is huge. It will take us forever to search it if we stick together."

"Better than two of us coming back and discovering that

the third one...*didn't*," Leo says darkly. "Think about it. This house is big, but it's also dangerous."

His words chill me to the core. "We'll stay together."

Will lowers his backpack to the ground with a *thud*. "Where should we start, then?"

I tap on the sketch I made of the house. "Right now, unexplained stuff has happened in three rooms: my room, the kitchen, and the ballroom."

Will nods slowly as if he's trying to process this. "So maybe there's a connection between those rooms?"

"That's what I thought!" I exclaim. "But if there is, I haven't found it yet. I'm hoping that whatever this opens"—I fish the skeleton key out of my pocket and hold it up—"will have some answers."

"Ahhh, the key to the secret door," Will murmurs as he takes the key from my hand. "That would be awesome."

"As awesome as strep throat or a cavity," Leo mumbles.

I side-eye him. "I don't want to wander around this place any more than you do, but there's no choice."

"Fine. I'm ready, then." Leo kicks his sneakers off, cracks his knuckles, and starts stretching his neck from side to side. He looks like he's about to enter a boxing ring.

"What are you doing?" Will asks, his blue eyes lit up with amusement.

"And you claim to be a tiptoe expert. Sneakers are loud on wood floors. I'm preparing to *quietly* search the house." He looks down at our feet. "If you don't want Dad to hear us sneaking around, you guys should do the same."

Laughing, I kick my shoes off too. Will does the same.

"Dad is probably having the meeting in the dining room. We should stay away from there for now," I suggest.

"Let's start in the ballroom, then," Leo says. "It's a mess still, and there's nowhere to sit, really, anyway, so I don't think Dad will go up there."

I meet Will's eyes. "Are you okay with that? I mean, I know it probably isn't your favorite idea."

"I'll be fine."

His tone is flat. I haven't been around Will that much, but I know that didn't sound like him. He's scared.

"You don't have to," I add. "Leo and I could go up and then you could help with the rest of the house."

"No, I want to. Can't be scared of that room forever."

If Will were Erica, I'd give him a hug right now. He's not though, and it might be weird. Not just because he's a boy—boys deserve hugs when they're worried too—but mostly because we haven't known each other as long as Erica and I have. Maybe he doesn't even like hugs. Some people don't.

Instead of hugging him, I pat his shoulder. It's more

223

awkward than I meant it to be, so I stop. Clearing my throat uncomfortably, I crack the door open. The hall is quiet. I inhale deeply and step out before any of us can change our minds.

CHAPTER THIRTY-SEVEN

The ballroom is darker than I expected. Thick black clouds slowly drift in front of the sun and stop, setting my nerves on edge. Hopefully there isn't another storm brewing. I wouldn't be surprised, though. Seems like that's all it does in Michigan.

Will stands just inside the doorway. His hands are balled up at his sides, and his jaw looks clenched.

"You okay?" I ask.

He smiles tightly. "Yup. Just taking a second."

Leo has wandered down into the far end of the room. I stop by Mom's destroyed boxes, careful not to step on any glass. It looks just as bad as it did last night. The remains of her mixer are crushed beneath the thickest part of the limb, and everything is covered in leaves, glass, and splinters of wood. It makes me sad all over again.

"Wow," Will breathes. "This is bad."

Will looks up through the broken window. Beyond the plastic that's fluttering with the breeze, the shadow of a tree sways back and forth. "The limbs of the tree hang over the house, so there really isn't any way to prove that this wasn't just an accident."

"I know. That's what my parents think. But get this, right before it happened, a new message showed up on the typewriter."

"What?" Will asks incredulously. "What did it say?"

"I'm not sure, to be honest. All the words ran together. Like, no spaces or anything. But the complete words were *poor home all bent*." Repeating the message makes me nervous all over again. I shake off the chill I can feel building despite the stifling air.

He pales. "That's...strange. The first message was so simple. *Get out*. This one sounds more like a riddle."

"I don't know. Seems pretty simple to me. If something is bent, it's messed up, right? Like that window. And *home* obviously means Woodmoor. I think the Shadow People are warning us that things will keep getting worse until we leave."

Will looks unconvinced. "I still think the wording is weird, but yeah. I guess that could be what it means." He goes quiet, his eyebrows pinched as if he's deep in thought. "Do you think we're doing the right thing, Ginny? I mean, maybe we should be calling the police instead of trying to handle this ourselves."

"And tell them what? That a ghost is after me?" I tease, growing serious when I notice the odd expression on his face. "What?"

"You think that's what the Shadow People are? Ghosts?"

The bumper sticker pops into my head again. Maybe the very first clue to Woodmoor Manor's mystery appeared before I even got out of the car.

"I don't know," I admit. I glance back down to the end of the room where Leo is walking around aimlessly. He stops by the far windows, looks out, and shakes his head. "It's possible, right?"

"Anything is possible. This house is old, and there have been a lot of guests over the years; there's no way people haven't died here."

I shiver despite the muggy air. "I don't like thinking about that. What if someone died *in* one of these rooms. What if their spirit or whatever doesn't know how to leave?"

"Or *want* to leave," he counters.

Trying not to think about that possibility, I refocus on the search. There has to be something we're missing. A hidden door. A clock that opens into a secret passageway. A tunnel beneath the house. Something that my key opens.

And, once it's opened, I'll learn more. I'll know more. Just like a good detective.

"In *Hickory Dickory Dock,* the detective is trying to find a thief," I tell them. "He carefully searches even basic things like the student's backpacks and discovers some of them were specially designed to hide stolen items."

"I take it that's an Agatha Christie novel?" Will asks, a smile tipping up the corner of his lips.

I nod, grinning. "Yup. We need to think like detectives. Examine everything!"

Leo appears beside me. "I *have* examined everything, and I'm starting to think we need to go back downstairs. This is just a big empty room."

Is it? If this is just a big empty room, then why did Will's brother see something in here all those years ago? And why did I barely escape an entire army of shadows?

I pull the key out of my shorts pocket and show it to him again. "You might be right, but let's all take a different side of the room just to be safe. Look for anything that sticks out—a door or a crack in the wall where there shouldn't be one—something unusual. Anything could be a clue right now!"

He points down to the opposite end of the ballroom. "I already checked out the door on the far wall. It just goes into a short hallway with a bathroom in it. Nothing else."

"No stairwell?" I ask.

He shakes his head. "Nope. Looks like the door we came in is the only entrance and exit for this room."

"Maybe the key isn't to a door?" Will suggests. "Like, what if there's a locked cabinet somewhere in the house."

"Maybe," I say, but I don't feel optimistic. I already searched the entire second floor by myself, and none of the cabinets even had locks on them. They also didn't have anything interesting inside.

I walk over to the other side of the room. It's the same pretty much, just a row of windows and a few fold-up chairs scattered here and there. Each window has a wooden bench built into the wall beneath it. We have a bench like that in our entryway back home. You can use it to sit while you're putting your shoes on, but it also opens up into storage. Mom keeps umbrellas and stuff like that in ours. Maybe these open too?

I place my fingers beneath the edge of a bench and tug upward, gasping when it creaks open. "Hey! These benches open!"

Leo and Will immediately pick different windows and open the benches beneath them. Meanwhile, I dig through the stuff in mine. "Um, this is mostly fabric. Tablecloths, I think?"

"Same here," Will calls out. "Also, some candlesticks. Didn't your dad say they use this room for events sometimes?"

"Yeah. He mentioned wedding receptions. I guess that explains the tablecloths." I lower the lid of my bench, noticing that Leo is quiet. He's crouched down in front of his bench, looking inside. "Is there something in there?"

He turns to face me. "Yup. I think you're gonna want to see this."

Rushing over, I kneel down at his side. The bench is filled with pictures—framed black-and-white photos. I pick one up and look into the eyes of the man in the center. He's older and balding and his face is filled with what Mom would call "happy wrinkles," the kind a person gets around their eyes and mouth from smiling a lot. Is this the millionaire Dad was talking about? The man who built Woodmoor?

I scrape my brain for his name but come up with nothing. Actually, now that I think about it, I don't remember Dad ever telling me his name. Strange, because Dad is really into history. Usually he tells me too much, not too little.

Leo flips the frame over to reveal a scribble of something on the faded brown paper backing. "J. B. Dottinger. It's written on the back of the frame."

"I've heard of him. He built this house," Will says, confirming my suspicion.

"So, he lived here then?" I ask.

"I guess. I don't remember much from the tour I went on,

but I remember that name. He was super rich and built this place for his wife, mostly."

I lift another frame. This one holds a photograph of a woman with dark hair and eyes. She's younger in this picture than J. B. was in his. A baby is perched on her lap, and a smile graces her delicate face. "This must be her. Annette Dottinger," I say, flipping the picture over to reveal the name on the back.

The next photo is of the same woman. She's older, though, and this time instead of holding a baby, Annette is standing in a cluster of trees and proudly displaying what looks like a poster. Her mouth is drawn into the biggest, brightest smile possible. I squint at the text on it, desperately trying to make out the words.

"I think that says *Woodmoor, 1937*," Leo says from over my shoulder. "Look at the little squares on it. I think she might be holding the floor plan for this house."

I scan the picture, noticing that there's a shovel held up in her other hand, and in the distance, the same eerie tree line my eyes were drawn to the day we arrived at Woodmoor. This picture must've been taken here, before the house was built.

"Wow. She looks so...proud. And excited. Annette must have really been into this place," I say, gingerly handing the picture to Will so he can get a closer look.

I keep digging. It's the very last photograph in the pile

that takes my breath away—a shot of the ballroom we're standing in. There's at least a hundred people in the picture, some smiling, some dancing, and more than a few holding glasses of clear liquid up in the air. And sitting in a chair on the edge of the photo is a frail-looking woman wearing a ball gown. A very *familiar* ball gown adorned with sequins.

My mouth drops open. I scour the woman's face, realizing that although she's much thinner in this picture, there's no doubt that it's Annette Dottinger. My gaze lingers on her face. It's totally different from the picture with the shovel. The smile is there, but it's weaker. Less excited and more...tired? Her eyes are sunken, and her skeletal body is little more than jutting bones covered with sequins.

"I think... I think this is the ball gown that the mannequin in my room is wearing," I say, my voice quivering with the possibility. "Doesn't it look like it?"

Leo narrows his eyes on the photograph. "I can't remember, Gin. Maybe?"

I shove all the other frames back in the bench and close it. My heart is pounding, and my knees feel wobbly. "We have to go check."

We quickly head back downstairs. Despite the fact that it's sunny outside, the hallways are dim. I feel jumpy, like every room we walk past could have something hiding in it.

Something waiting for us, for *me*. Bony hands ready to reach out and grab me... A shadow drifting closer and closer.

Stopping in my doorway, I do my best to take calming breaths. In and out. In and out. I hate looking at the mannequin, I hate even *thinking* about the mannequin, but the photograph clenched tightly in my hand could be our big break.

"Are you okay?" Will asks quietly.

I nod but don't speak. Truth is, I'm tired of being afraid to walk into this room! Tired of being afraid to walk down the hall or go to sleep! And right now, I'm extra afraid to face the mannequin again. I know what will happen if I don't, though.

Sensing my fear, Will stands shoulder-to-shoulder with me. "We'll do it together, okay?"

"Thank you," I whisper, hoping Will knows I'm not normally such a coward. But I've never had to deal with things this scary before. The most frightening parts about living in Chicago are things like bad traffic and clueless tourists in the summertime. "On three?"

"Sure." Will grins. "Three."

I laugh despite my nerves. "That's cheating."

He lifts one shoulder in a lopsided shrug. "Maybe, but it will get us in and out of that room faster. So, let's do this, *future Agatha Christie*."

His comment makes me stand up a little straighter. I'd do anything to be the next Agatha Christie, including this.

Chin lifted, I march into the room with Will at my side and Leo trailing behind us. It's even hotter than usual. The sun is streaming through the windows, making the air thick and sticky. Stopping in front of the mannequin, I shakily hold the frame up next to it. The goose bumps immediately return.

"It *is* the same dress," I whisper. I reach out and gingerly run a finger over the fabric. "So, I guess that means this belonged to Annette Dottinger."

"If you're right and that *is* her dress," Will begins, "then that could mean this was her room."

I consider this, an uncomfortable feeling rippling through me. Up until now, I hadn't really thought about whose room I was staying in. If it is Annette's room, then that means there's a solid chance that the connection between my room and the ballroom isn't hidden behind a secret mystery door... It's *Annette*.

CHAPTER THIRTY-EIGHT

Is she our ghost?

A memory breaks free—Dad's expression when I chose this room. It was uncertain, like he had something to say but decided against it. Now that I think about it, I wonder if he looked that way because he knows more than he let on.

I lift the picture up to the wall behind the mannequin a second time. The holes drilled through the corners of the frame match up perfectly with the ones in my wall. This photograph is *definitely* what was hanging here before.

"When I first picked this room, I wondered why there was no label for the ball gown. Since it's a display item and all," I say, flipping the picture back over and staring into the face of Annette Dottinger.

"Have you guys heard anything about Annette?" I ask.

"Like, are there any Shadow People legends that mention her specifically?"

"I never heard of her until we found the pictures," Leo admits.

Will lowers down onto my bed. I've watched him a lot lately. I know his eyes are the color of a summer sky, and his cheeks are dotted in tiny brown freckles. I know he's serious but sweet, and that he's into books, like me. I also know that he's nervous right now. I can tell because his hands are knotted so tightly in his lap that his knuckles are white.

I sit down next to him, half afraid to ask what is rumbling around in his head. He didn't even look this nervous when we discovered the message on the typewriter. "What is it?"

"It might not be anything," he says quietly.

"Dude, you look like you're going to puke. It's something for sure." Leo stops pacing and sits down on the rug, cross-legged. He looks like a giant, folded-up grasshopper.

Will blinks at me. His expression is apologetic. "It's just that before I left the tour and went into the ballroom with my brother, I had to listen to this little introduction talk about the house. That's how I knew Dottinger built it for his wife."

"And?" I nudge.

"I think they said something about her. About her *dying*."

A trickle of fear pulses through me. I tell myself to get it together, that the future Agatha Christie cannot get scared this easily. "Mmm, okay. Why didn't you say anything about this before?"

"I didn't think it was important. When we first started trying to figure all this stuff out, I wasn't really thinking about the Shadow People being *ghosts*."

"What did you think they were? Monsters?" Leo asks, letting out a hoot. I shush him, and he rolls his eyes at me.

Will shrugs. "Honestly? Yeah. The Hitchhikers are supposedly creatures, so I guess I kinda thought the Shadow People were something like that."

My eyes flick down to the picture in my lap. Even though Annette's smile isn't as big in this photo as it is in the one of her with the floor plan, it's still there. How could someone who seemed happy end up the kind of ghost who haunts people?

"Do you remember anything else?" I prod. "From the tour, I mean?"

Will shakes his head miserably.

"Then there's no real proof." Leo stretches his legs out. I scoot my own feet away from his. The last thing I want touching me right now is his nasty socks. "The picture is a great start, but can we really be sure she's the one haunting this place?"

I look from the mannequin to the mirror, a theory forming. "Maybe. Will's brother saw a *woman* shadow in the ballroom. And I saw a face in my mirror that looked like a woman. That's a connection right there! Then there's the fact that a lot of the bad things that have happened since we got to Woodmoor were in my room. I thought it was because the ghost was targeting me, but maybe that's not it at all."

"Maybe it's because this is her room," Will says.

"Exactly. If you put those clues together with this picture," I hold up the frame, shaking it for effect. "One *could* conclude that the ghost is in fact Annette Dottinger!"

"*One could conclude?*" Leo mocks. "You really gotta read some other stuff. You're starting to sound like some kind of old-fashioned detective."

I bend forward and punch him in the shoulder. "Shut up. You know I'm right. This could be huge!"

"Okay. Well, if we're assuming that the ghost is Annette Dottinger, what now?" Will asks.

"Well, for starters I guess we need to find out how she died." My stomach hollows out at the thought. I don't usually feel this way when I'm reading mystery novels, like I'm about to throw up, but this is different. Ghosts seem a lot scarier than humans, even if those humans are making terrible choices.

"Then we need to see how the other clues fit together—if they do," I continue. "Annette looks happy in those pictures. Mostly, anyway." I think back on the picture of her in the ballroom, how her smile had shrunken almost as much as her body. "If she is the ghost haunting Woodmoor, then something really awful must have happened after she moved in here." I mean, I don't know much about ghosts, but I don't think they go looking for revenge just *because*."

"You're totally right. On this show I watch, er... I mean, I only watch it if nothing else is on," Leo pauses and clears his throat awkwardly. "They investigate paranormal stuff. Almost all the time, the ghost had something to be upset about."

I giggle behind my hand. Leo doesn't just watch that show when nothing else is on. At least three times a week, high-pitched shrieks filter through the wall that separates our rooms. Most of the time it's the people in the show, but sometimes it's my chicken of a brother.

"The big question is, what could Annette Dottinger have had to be upset about?" I ask. "They were rich and living in a mansion." *Money doesn't buy happiness.* Dad says that all the time.

"That's just it, though," Leo interrupts. He leans back so he's propped up on his elbows, legs crossed at the knees. "Anyone can seem happy. Doesn't mean they are. Annette Dottinger could've had a secret, something that turned her into an angry, restless spirit after death. Maybe it was something that happened while she was alive, or maybe it was that she died some horrible death. Figuring out her secret might be the key to solving this."

The word key reminds me of the skeleton key in my pocket. I feel for the outline of it, wondering if I'll ever find what it opens, and if the door it matches holds any useful secrets or just more dust bunnies and old pictures.

"Well, whatever her problem was, we need to figure it out fast. You're supposed to be back in Chicago tomorrow!" Will says, frustrated.

My shoulders droop.

"Yeah, about that. I'm, um...not going." The words taste bitter in my mouth.

"What do you mean you're not going? There's still time!"

I shake my head. "There isn't. I'm not a ghost expert or anything, but I think it might take longer than one day to convince this spirit to leave Woodmoor for good."

His eyebrows jump. "Hold up, I thought you just wanted proof of the haunting so you could get out of here. Did something change?"

"Sort of. I overheard my parents talking and...it's just that they're so worried about this job. They really need it to go well. But if I just run away like everyone else does, it won't matter what my Dad does to Woodmoor. It will still lose money."

Will's expression softens. "I didn't think about that."

"It's okay," I say, trying to sound convincing. It isn't okay, but I need Will focused on solving the mystery, not feeling bad for me. "We still need to work fast because the ghost is getting angrier and angrier. The limb that smashed the window last night could have really hurt someone."

I clap my hands down on the tops of my legs, feeling accomplished. Funny, since I haven't actually accomplished anything yet. Still, we've had our first big breakthrough! Annette could be our ghost, and if she is, the first part of this mystery is solved. This is one of those moments in a book where you start to think the detective has things under control.

I do have things under control...right?

CHAPTER THIRTY-NINE

"Ooh, we can't forget about that song you heard," Leo mentions, pulling at a stray string in his sock. When it comes loose, he tosses it onto my lap. I swipe it off and scramble away. I wonder if Agatha had brothers to deal with. Probably not. "We still don't know what that was, and it's probably important."

He's not wrong. I didn't imagine that song. If the ghost wanted me to hear it, then it must be important.

"Wait! Will, didn't you say something about an older couple that runs a bed-and-breakfast close to the bookstore?" I ask, adrenaline spiking in me. "Yes! I remember now. You said they love spooky things and are obsessed with Woodmoor. Couldn't we go try and talk to them? They might know what that song was!"

Will runs a hand through his hair. "They'll talk to anyone, but I don't think they're worth talking to."

"Why? Old people like old music! Plus, if they're always buying books about this place, then surely they would know something."

"They sound like weirdos," Leo chimes in.

"They *are* weirdos." Will stands up and walks to the window. "They're nice and all, but last summer, the husband told everyone in town he was abducted by aliens, who made him eat cheeseburgers for two days."

My adrenaline slows to a trickle, then fizzes out entirely. "Aliens?"

Leo perks up. "Cheeseburgers?"

A bubble of laughter bursts from Will. "Dude. All you heard out of what I just said was *cheeseburgers*?"

"That's not *all* I heard," Leo answers sheepishly.

Riiiight.

Will refocuses on me. "Unfortunately, yeah. Aliens. Like I said, they're really nice, but I'm sure they'd tell you anything you want to hear. That's the problem."

Ugh. *Unreliable.* That's what Agatha would call witnesses like them. It's great to interview people who actually saw something that might help you, but it sounds like this couple isn't very trustworthy. They could give us bad information and that would be worse than no information at all.

"Well, that's it then." Leo jumps up and begins stretching out his legs. "Looks like it's séance time!"

"Slow down." I reach out and snag his ankle, pulling my brother back down to the floor. "We don't need to jump straight to the séance."

"You wanna try to get a ride into town with Mom? The internet works a lot better there," my brother suggests.

"Nah," I wave off the idea. "We still have a secret weapon, and it's right here in the house."

Leo stares at me quizzically. "Leftover pizza?"

"How would leftover pizza be a secret weapon? Ugh. No, Leo. I'm talking about books!" I turn to Will. "You brought some from the store, right?"

"Yup." Will heads for the door. "My bag is in Leo's room. Wanna go through them in there?"

I snort. "Now that we know my room is, like, haunted headquarters, *absolutely*."

We follow him into the hallway. I take a deep breath, savoring the slightly cooler air. My room—er, Annette's room—really is a sauna.

Will takes the books out of his bag and gently stacks them in the center of the room. I love that he's so careful with them. "I didn't really know what we'd need, so I just brought a little of everything."

I check out the options. There's a couple of books on Michigan ghost legends, one about Saugatuck, and two about the history of the county we are in. "Hmm. Maybe we should all just pick one and start digging for information on Annette."

Leo dives for one of the ghost books. Of course he does. With my luck, he's planning to scour it for proof that we need to hold a séance.

Will snags the book on Saugatuck, which leaves me with the two books on Allegan County. I pick up the first one, crack it open, and, out of habit, take a quick sniff of the pages. As usual, the smell puts a smile on my face. It's woodsy and a little bit sweet. I wish everything smelled like books.

"Did you just smell that book?" Leo asks, wrinkling his nose.

"Maybe," I fire back. "Books are one of the best smells in the world."

"Nerd," he responds, climbing up onto his bed.

I stick my tongue out at him, then prop myself up against the wall. Will has settled into the corner and is already focused on his book. He turns a page, then turns it back again to reread something. I can't help but smile at how serious he is. Will is great. He's also probably the only thing about this place I'll miss when we finally make it back home.

Skimming the pages of my book, I stop every time I

see Woodmoor mentioned. There are several pictures of the mansion, including a few that we saw upstairs in the ballroom. There's also another one of Annette, posing with the shovel. She's grinning and holding it to the ground. There's a handwritten inscription at the bottom of the photo that reads: *Breaking Ground on Woodmoor Manor*. Running a finger over the glossy photo, I imagine her excitement.

I continue flipping pages and scanning paragraphs until my eyelids get heavy. Just when I think I'm going to have to take a break, my eyes snag on a cluster of words.

...fell into ruins after tragedy struck.

Tragedy? My heart skips a beat, then another. Jumping forward a few lines, I start reading again, groaning when I realize it's all about the mansion falling apart and not about the tragedy.

Will's head snaps up. "What's wrong?"

"This chapter mentions a tragedy, but it doesn't say what it was."

He sits up straighter. "A tragedy at Woodmoor?"

I nod, swallowing hard. "I think so. It says that the mansion *'fell into ruins after tragedy struck.'*"

Peeking at Leo, I startle to see that his eyes are already fixed on me. They're worried, and his skin, usually bronzed from too many hours on the basketball court, is growing paler by the second. I inhale sharply, unnerved. Unlike Will, Leo isn't a serious person. He likes to joke around, and it takes a *lot* to upset him. Either he ate a whole bag of spicy Cheetos and then drank two Cokes again, or he just read something scary in that ghost book.

"What is it?" I ask. "Did your book say something about a tragedy too?"

"Yes. And it has to do with Annette."

Will and I clamor up onto the bed. I kick the blankets away from my sticky body so I can spread out.

Leo flips his book around so we can see the pages. There's an image of Woodmoor sitting beneath an eerie full moon, and beside it, a second photograph—this one of Annette Dottinger. Unlike the pictures we uncovered in the ballroom, she isn't smiling. Her gaunt face is angled away from the camera, and her mouth is slightly downturned. I search the rest of the photo for evidence of where it was taken. My jaw drops when I notice the wallpaper surrounding the cluster of windows at her back.

"Oh my gosh! I think this is the sunroom!" I point at the wallpaper. Even in black and white, I recognize the pattern. It's not a perfect match, but it's close. "Dad said when they renovated this house the first time, they used old pictures to make the inside as authentic as possible."

"That would make sense," Leo says gloomily. "Because according to this book, Annette got really sick right after Woodmoor was completed and spent most of her time in that room."

"How sick?" Will asks. "Like a cold, or something worse?"

Without speaking, Leo flips the book around a second time. Half the page is taken up with a picture of a tombstone bearing the initials *A.E.D.*

He reads aloud from the caption. "'Annette Elizabeth Dottinger died two short months after construction on Woodmoor Manor was completed.'"

CHAPTER FORTY

When I finally tear my eyes off the tombstone, Leo is staring at me again.

"Apparently Annette was diagnosed with cancer while Woodmoor was still being built, so J. B. had the sunroom added to her bedroom so she could get sun even when she couldn't go outside."

I let out a gasp. No wonder my room is always so hot! The sunroom was created specifically to keep it bright and warm.

"She only got to live here two months?" Will presses. "Wow. That's...sad."

The haunting image of Annette's wafer-thin body in the sequined ball gown comes to mind. No wonder she was one of the only people sitting down in the picture we found. She probably didn't have the energy to stand.

Sadness pricks at me as I imagine her growing sicker while Woodmoor was coming together. Based on the smile she wore in the photo with the floor plans, this house was her dream home.

My mind is reeling. "If this is true, then Annette Dottinger *definitely* had a reason to haunt Woodmoor after she died."

Will sets his book down in his lap. "For sure. If Annette's spirit feels cheated, then that would explain why she's haunting anyone who visits here. They're enjoying the house she couldn't enjoy." He turns to face me, a wariness in his expression I don't like seeing. "And Ginny was enjoying *her* room."

"The same room she might have died in," Leo adds, gravely. "This says the cancer moved fast, and she couldn't get out of bed at the end."

I look back down at the photograph in Leo's book. The gloomy, wilted expression on Annette's face is awful. So is the thought that she may've died in the room I've been sleeping in every night.

"That's why my room seems the most haunted." I lick at my dry lips, wishing I'd picked any other room that first day. "It also explains why the house ended up in ruins. If Annette started haunting Woodmoor right after she passed away, I don't blame her husband for not wanting to stay here."

"Yeah, but even if she *didn't* start haunting it right away, he probably didn't want to be here anymore. Look at this." Leo sets the book down and taps on the page. It's a picture of some bricks. There are words etched into the face of them.

To Annette, 1937

My mind flashes back to the first time I walked up to the front door of this house. I remember seeing an inscription in the brick, just to the left of the entryway. I hadn't thought much of it at the time, didn't even take time to read it because of how upset I was, but now I realize that might've been a big, *big* mistake.

"Woodmoor would have reminded him of her. Maybe so much that he couldn't stand to live here after she was gone," I say, my voice hoarse with sadness. I never expected to feel anything but anger over what the ghost has put me through, but in the past hour, all of that has changed. I feel terrible for Annette, and even though he didn't die, just as bad for her husband. I get it now, totally understand why J. B. Dottinger was so desperate to escape the house he once adored, even if it ultimately meant letting it rot. What's the point of having a mansion if the person you love can't enjoy it with you?

Holding my hand out, I take Leo's book and start flipping through the pages. "Did you see anything in here about the kitchen or the ballroom? Because that still doesn't make sense to me. Why would she haunt those two rooms if she died in my room?"

"I didn't, but I've been thinking about that." Leo swipes the back of his arm across a bead of sweat trickling down his forehead and sighs. "Remember when we moved those boxes into the ballroom for Dad? Didn't he say something about it being built because Annette Dottinger wanted to entertain people?"

I *think* I remember something about that, but I was so scared that night I can't be sure. "Why would that matter?"

Leo slaps a hand to his forehead. "I really need to get you guys watching *Spirit Hunters*. Seriously. If there's anything I've learned from that show, it's that what the ghost wanted when he or she was alive *always* matters."

"So, you're saying you think Annette Dottinger is haunting the rooms she liked the most?" Will asks.

"Ding, ding, ding! Those rooms were custom built just for her," Leo responds.

Huh. Based on what we know so far, Leo's theory works. Annette Dottinger spent most of her time in my room because she was sick. She also had big dreams of hosting all her friends and family in her gleaming, new ballroom. Still doesn't explain the kitchen, though...

Just then, a strange sound echoes down the hallway. *Music.* I leap off the bed and stand at the doorway, heart hammering in my chest. Hesitantly, I place an ear to the wood. The words are muffled, but the tune is clear enough to send a bolt of fear into my core. It's *the* song...the one from behind the ticking.

Nooooo.

"What is that?" Will asks.

I spin around to face him, legs quaking. "You hear it too?"

"Yeah. It sounds like carnival music, maybe?"

Letting out a sigh of relief that I'm not the only one who can hear it this time, I crack open Leo's door. The hallway is darker than it was when we came in. Glancing back at the window, I notice why. Dark clouds have moved in, eclipsing the sun.

"Is that *the* song?" Leo asks. He scrambles to the edge of the bed, the book toppling from his lap to the floor. "The one you were talking about?"

"It is." The first drops of rain begin hitting the windows. Thunder groans in the distance. "I have a bad feeling about this, guys."

"That makes two of us." Will edges toward the door. "I know we should probably go check it out, but I'm really not excited about that idea."

Leo springs up. "I'll go first. You two aren't trained for this kind of stuff."

I'd laugh if I wasn't so worried. Leo isn't trained for this either. He's watched some dumb ghost show a few times, and now he thinks he's an expert. This reminds me of when we were little, and I discovered a wasp nest high in the corner of our front porch. My brother tried to get rid of it himself and took a big stick and poked it until the wasps spewed out. He got stung six times.

I tug on his sleeve to slow him down.

"Remember the tree limb," I warn him. Leo makes me crazy sometimes, but he's still my brother. That means I can't watch him run headfirst into danger. And this ghost... She's dangerous. At least she is until we figure out exactly what she wants and give it to her. "We need to take this slow. And...together."

He nods in understanding. Maybe he's remembering the welts the wasps left behind, or maybe he's just listening to me for once. Whatever the reason is, I'm grateful.

Motioning for them to follow me, I creep into the hall. I turn left and head toward the servants' wing but stop when I realize the music is growing quieter.

"Other way," I whisper, nearly crashing into Will as I spin around. When we reach the doorway of my parent's room, I pause again. "It's coming from in there."

"But Mom is gone...and Dad is downstairs, right?" Leo asks. His voice quivers.

Even without me answering, my brother knows he's correct. He probably also knows that means the person playing that music isn't a human. Not anymore, anyway.

It's Annette. It has to be.

I reach out slowly and touch the doorknob. It's icy, frigid as the air the night I saw the shadow drift through my room.

The music grows louder, and the notes become distorted. If songs could melt, this would be the sound they would make. I rub my clammy hands together, wishing I had a plan. Then again, it seems like the only time I've made progress on this mystery was when I *didn't* have a plan, when things just played out the way the ghost wanted them to. Like when I came face-to-face with the mannequin in the middle of the night, or when the ghost appeared in my mirror. Even discovering the typewriter messages just...happened.

I consider this, wondering if trying to force this mystery into an Agatha-shaped mold might've been my biggest problem this whole time. I've been so focused on the skeleton key and doing things the way I think she would've done them that I never figured out what *my* way is. Because of that, I missed the clues that mattered most—the haunted house bumper sticker, my baking hot room, the family who built this house...

the woman who died here and keeps appearing in shadows and mirrors.

It's time to stop trying to be the future Agatha Christie and instead be the future Ginny Anderson.

Without a final, calming breath, I toss the door open. The music stops. I blink in shock as the curtains billow out as if they're filled with helium, then slowly lower back down. Turning around, I see where the music was coming from—the record player. It's bigger than the ones I've seen in pictures, and there's a metal crank jutting out from the side.

"A gramophone," Will whispers. "There was one for sale in the antique shop last summer." He reaches out and gently lifts the needle, then reads the name on the record it was playing. "'In the Good Old Summertime.'"

"Good old summertime?" Leo snorts. "More like, terrible, haunted summertime."

A jagged bolt of lightning flashes across the gray sky. I look around the room nervously. "Do you think she was in here?"

"I do, don't you?" Will answers. "I think she wanted us to come in here and discover this record."

Leo's face drains of color. He looks like a cardboard cutout of himself, rigid and ashen. "Do you think she's in here...*now*?"

Movement draws my eyes to the space behind Leo. A

ripple of smoke, like someone just blew out a candle. Only there's no candle. I blink to clear my eyes, gasping when I realize the smoke is no longer smoke, but a shadow—a woman shadow.

Annette.

She hovers at Leo's back, her piercing red eyes fixed on me and her mouth open in a grotesque scream.

Don't. Turn. Around. I mouth to my brother. His eyes widen. Will grabs my hand and squeezes. Annette's shadow reaches out, the gnarled arms growing closer and closer to Leo. I'm so scared I can't move. Can't think.

A strong breeze suddenly rips through the room, slamming the door shut. I scream, then immediately grasp the knob and start trying to turn it. It won't budge.

We're locked in.

CHAPTER FORTY-ONE

With panic in his eyes, Leo lowers one shoulder and says, "That's it. I'm gonna break it down."

Before I can even try to stop him, he barrels forward. Just before impact, the door flies wide, revealing my father's shocked face. He leaps out of the way, tugging the man beside him out of Leo's path. Apparently, my brother had too much steam going to stop because he hurtles through the doorway and crashes straight into the wall. With a muffled *hrmph*, he sinks to the ground.

"Leo!" Dad says, helping him up. "Are you okay?"

My brother rubs his shoulder, nodding sheepishly. "I think so."

Whirling around, I scan the area where the Annette-shaped shadow was. It's gone. The feeling is still here, though. The horrible icy feeling of dread.

I turn back to the man standing beside Dad. He's got salt-and-pepper hair and a wrinkled-up forehead. He's also got a *very* concerned look on his face.

"What on earth is going on?" Dad asks, forcing a tone that's supposed to sound pleasant but totally doesn't. I'm not surprised. Mom *did* tell us not to disrupt his meeting.

Will looks at me expectantly. I start to answer, then realize I have absolutely no good explanation for what just happened. I'm also still holding his hand. I drop it quickly. Will clears his throat nervously, then tries to lean back against the wall. Instead, he stumbles against the nightstand, catches himself, and folds his arms over his chest like none of it ever happened.

Awkward.

Dad looks unsettled. "I need answers, guys. We were just finishing up when we heard screaming up here."

"Music, too," the man adds, a glimmer of curiosity in his eyes.

Lifting the record, Will pulls a smile to his face. It's his bookstore smile I think, the one he must give customers when he's trying to make them happy. "We found this old record, and I guess we just wanted to hear it. Sorry if we were too loud."

Although my father's face stays blank, the man he's with tilts his head to the side, his expression a mixture of surprise and curiosity. "Well, well, well. Look at what you've found.

I'm impressed you kids knew how to operate this thing." He gestures to the gramophone, which we most definitely did not know how to use.

"Oh, uh, yeah. Took a little figuring out for sure," Will fibs. "Do you know anything about this? The song was... interesting."

By *interesting* I assume he means *creepy*, because it was.

"This isn't necessary, Robert," my father interrupts. "My daughter and her friend are very...inquisitive. But we have other matters to attend to, so I know they'd be fine with researching the record on their own." He punctuates this last bit with a stern look in my direction. Yikes.

"Nonsense," the man says, pulling my attention back to him. "I'm happy to answer questions. I've been a co-owner of Woodmoor for many years, and despite everything that has happened, I'm still proud of this place."

His comment sticks in my head. *Despite everything that has happened.* Is he acknowledging that Woodmoor is haunted? Or maybe he's just talking about all the money they've lost. Either way, he seems willing to help, which we can't turn down.

"Thank you." Leo edges closer, still rubbing at his shoulder.

The man—Robert—smiles. It's warm and genuine. "Call me Robert. Please. That record was part of the original owner's collection. Annette Dottinger. According to reports, she played it for hours, was even planning a big event in the ballroom based on it. That's why we leave it displayed on the gramophone."

My ears prick up. "Wait...an event in the *ballroom*?"

"Oh yes. A very fancy one. We don't know all the details, of course, but J. B. Dottinger kept a ledger of upcoming events that is still in our collection. He had the date for the big event listed in there under the title 'Good Old Summertime.' Was supposed to happen this very month, I think." Robert glances wistfully out the window. "Unfortunately, poor Annette passed away before they could host it."

I look at the record in Will's hands, wondering if we might have just uncovered why Annette's ghost has been playing that song. "So, the event was canceled?"

"There's no documentation that shows it happened, so I presume it was. Her husband didn't fare so well after she died, so I can't imagine he would have hosted it without her."

"Thanks for the information. We'll put this away." Will holds the record up.

Robert nods and heads for the doorway. Just before walking out, he turns back to Dad. "I'll get those electricians back to make the repairs tomorrow. Perhaps keep the lights out in the kitchen until then, just to be safe? Faulty wiring is nothing to be messed with."

"Absolutely. I'll walk you out." Dad follows him out the door, then turns back and mouths, *We'll talk later.*

When they're finally far enough away that I can't hear their voices anymore, I slump against the wall and slide down to the ground. "I can't believe it."

"What? The fact that I almost died at the hands of a ghost just now?" Leo asks.

I laugh despite the fear still pulsing through me. Even if I never have one good memory of Woodmoor, the image of my brother flailing through that open door will always make me smile. "Yeah, that and the summertime party thing."

Will sits down next to me. "What are you thinking?"

"That it can't be a coincidence. Annette Dottinger was planning a big party that was supposed to happen this month—a party that was inspired by the song she's been playing since I got here. Those things have to be connected, right?"

"Totally," Leo agrees. "But I guess I still don't really know what to do with that."

"Me, either," says Will. He gently sets the record back on the player and turns to face me. "Definitely not a coincidence, though."

Maybe there are no coincidences when it comes to hauntings. Maybe there are just two categories for stuff: clues and not clues. "In the Good Old Summertime" definitely seems like a clue.

Robert's comment about the electricity suddenly pops into my head. "Remember how we were trying to figure out how the kitchen is connected? Maybe it isn't. If there really is an electrical problem in there, then I guess the light bulbs bursting was just a..."

Red herring.

I laugh to myself.

"A what?" Leo prompts. "Jeez, Gin. Start finishing your sentences, please!"

"No, wait! Let me," Will says with a cheeky grin. Then he starts talking again, using the most dramatic and ridiculous voice I've ever heard. I think he's trying to sound British. "The kitchen light bulbs exploding were nothing but a red herring. Am I right, Miss Scarlet?"

I lift an eyebrow, impressed. "How did you know Clue is my favorite board game?"

He laughs. It's a belly laugh, the kind that echoes off the walls and makes everyone else smile. "Just a hunch."

"Hellooooo," Leo says, waving his hand between us. "Could we get back to the exploding light bulbs? What do they have to do with fish?"

"Fish?" Will and I ask at the same time.

263

"Um, red herring?" Leo repeats, his face pinched. "Your words, not mine."

"Oh, sorry. A red herring is a fake clue," I explain, trying not to laugh. Of course, my brother would think a red herring is just a fish. Knowing his stomach, he was probably imagining it battered and fried.

"So, the light bulbs breaking in the kitchen over and over again meant nothing?" he continues.

"Nothing except they need a better electrician for this place," I answer with a snort.

Will's phone makes a chirping sound. He slides it from his pocket and groans. "My dad is five minutes away. Guess that means my time is up."

"So fast?" I ask. "Can't you stay just a little longer? We're so close!"

Will taps an imaginary watch on his wrist. "I know, but he likes to stay on a schedule, remember? Plus, I forgot he booked a fishing guide for us this evening, and it's already four thirty. He's been looking forward to it for weeks, so I can't cancel. It would ruin his whole trip."

"But the storm," I start, abruptly stopping when I notice the sun is back out. The black clouds and rolling thunder seem to have just...vanished.

Will looks from the window to me. "It's gone. Weird."

Pfft. Weird doesn't begin to cover the things happening here at Woodmoor.

"I'll walk you out." I walk out the door, then pause and look at Leo, who is still holding his shoulder. "And I'll get you an ice pack."

We're halfway down the main stairwell when Will stops walking.

"What's wrong?" I ask, then realize I know the answer. "Ugh. Your books are still in Leo's room. I'll just run back up and get them."

"No, it's not that. You might need those, so keep them here." He glances back up the stairs, then back at me. "I'm just worried."

"About what?"

"You," he says quietly, refusing to meet my eyes.

I'm speechless. I could be wrong, but it seems like Will is admitting he...*cares* about me?

"I just feel bad leaving when this isn't totally fixed yet," he amends.

"It's okay. We are a lot closer to solving all this than we were this morning, thanks to you." My hands are shaking. Hopefully Will doesn't notice.

"Thanks to the books, not me."

"Still." I reach out for a fist bump or something, then

immediately stop when I remember the awkward shoulder pat from before. I don't want to repeat that. This time, though, Will doesn't hesitate. He hugs me.

"Be careful, Ginny," he says as he pulls away. "You know that older couple we were talking about before? They're weird and all, but they said something one time that kinda stuck with me."

"Do I even want to know what that was?" I ask.

He shoots me an apologetic look. "Probably not, but I'm gonna tell you anyway. They said the more a spirit lost out on because of death, the more they have to be angry about. And Annette lost a *lot*."

"She did," I agree, my voice thick with sadness. "Now that I know all this, I feel bad for her." I think about the pictures of her breaking ground on Woodmoor, the dedication from her husband on the brick outside, and the dark, empty ballroom she once imagined would be filled with friends and family. I might have lost my writing workshop, but at least that's temporary. I can still go; just not this month. Annette Dottinger, though, she lost everything. *Permanently.*

I don't know if there's any way to fix that for her.

CHAPTER FORTY-TWO

By the time I get back upstairs, Leo is half asleep. He's draped over the bed in his room, the ghost book lying on his chest. I consider waking him up so we can keep brainstorming, but the dark circles under his eyes stop me. He must not be getting very good sleep these days either.

Instead, I head back to my room. It's quiet and feels more somber than it did before. I remember picking this space, thinking that I was really sticking it to my brother because it was the biggest room with the best bed and a whole private sunroom. Now I realize I might have caused this whole mess to begin with. I upset Annette Dottinger's spirit. I made her remember all the things she's missing and caused her to lash out at us. That means I need to be the one to make her happy again.

But how? I can't change the fact that she's gone and other

people are using her dream home. If that's why she wants revenge, then I'm doomed. There must be something else. Another way to make her happy...

I sit down on the bed and let my eyes close. My body feels heavy, exhausted from so many days of worrying. Settling into the darkness behind my eyelids, I tell myself I'll just take a five-minute break. Just five minutes to forget about the nightmare I've been living here at Woodmoor.

Then I fall asleep.

When I wake up, it's dark. I blink my eyes, confused and disoriented. What time is it? Did I sleep through dinner? I sit up and notice a slip of paper on my bed.

Hey, kiddo. We didn't want to wake you, so I put your dinner in the refrigerator. Just heat it up when you're ready. Love, Mom.

Setting the paper back down, I stretch out, then dig around in the blankets for my cell phone. When I find it, I gasp. It's nine o'clock! How did I sleep for over four hours? I scroll through my texts. Three from Will. One from Erica. And one from...Leo? I open his text, tapping my toe impatiently while it loads.

Sorry I cashed out. Check out the date.

There's a picture attached. It's a screenshot of a page from the ghost book. I use my thumb and forefinger to make it larger, my gaze immediately catching on the same photo that Leo showed Will and me earlier. Annette's grave. I scan the dates at the bottom, my jaw dropping when I realize what my brother wanted me to see—the date Annette died. I pull up the calendar on my phone and count the days. Eight. The anniversary of Annette Dottinger's death is only eight days away. That means Robert was right; the party she was planning to host was probably supposed to happen in June.

Walking to my door, I crack it open and look down the hall. Silent. Nothing but a random creak here and there, the house *settling* as Dad always says. Too bad he doesn't know what I do—that there's plenty of other reasons that houses make sounds. One of them being *ghosts*.

I tiptoe down to Leo's room, pausing outside his door. There's a sliver of light shining out from beneath it. Hopefully that means he's awake.

I give the knob a gentle turn and push the door open a few inches. Leo's bed is empty, and I can hear the shower running. Taking a few steps in, I spot what I came for—the ghost book. I pick it up and head back to my room.

Closing the door behind me, I climb up onto my bed and

crack the book open. It doesn't take long to find the chapter on Woodmoor because Leo dog-eared it. I study every picture of Annette, hoping to uncover a clue I didn't notice before. We know she's our ghost, but there's definitely evidence we're missing...the same evidence that might help me decide how to get her spirit to move on.

A pinch on the top of my thigh draws me away from the book. I shift on the bed until I can get my hand in my pocket, then dig around to see what's poking me. It's the skeleton key. I'd forgotten it was in there. I hold it up, wondering if the key was another red herring all along too. Maybe it's just a coincidence and has nothing to do with Annette, like the light bulbs exploding in the kitchen.

I'm staring at the little teeth on the end of the key when something Will said pushes its way into my brain. *Maybe it's not to a door.*

At the time, I didn't think much about that. I mean, I searched the whole second floor, so I know there aren't any mysterious locked cabinets or drawers here. On the first floor, the only cabinets are in the kitchen, and the library is lined with bookshelves, not drawers. If the key doesn't fit a door, a cabinet, or a drawer, what *does* it fit?

A box. The thought slips into my head so quickly I startle. The day Leo scared me with the speaking tube, I found a plastic box under my bed. Inside that was a smaller metal one. If I remember right, that metal box had a silver lock attached to it. A lock, but no key. At least not one that I saw.

Scrambling off my bed, I drop down to all fours and lift the dust ruffle. The plastic box is still there. I drag it out, then take off the lid. The metal box is nestled inside. I pick it up and examine the lock. I can't tell for sure, but it looks like the right size for the skeleton key I found.

Lining up the teeth of the key with the lock hole, I send a wish into the universe and push. It slides in easily. With a half turn, the lock pops open. I stare at it, stunned. All this time, the mystery keyhole was here, in my room?

I crack open the lid of the box. At first, I think it's filled with junk. Old yellowed papers are jammed deep inside. They're folded but wrinkled like someone crumpled them up and then tried to smooth them out. I know what that looks like because I've done it before with homework that didn't go well. Gently, I lift one of the papers and unfold it.

Flowers (from garden, perhaps?)
Music, live
Finger foods
Candles

I stop reading there. The list reminds me of the one my aunt made when she was planning my grandma and grandpa's fiftieth wedding anniversary.

Turning the paper over, I scour it for anything else. The back is blank. The other sheets of paper hold rough sketches of the ballroom. One of them shows small, round tables drawn in around what is labeled *dance floor*. There's a section for the band and one for a long table with food. Oh my gosh! This must've been her floor plan for the "Good Old Summertime" party! I wonder if the owners of Woodmoor even remember they have these. They probably put them in this box, stuffed them under the bed, and forgot about them.

The last few papers at the bottom of the box are different. Smaller, too. There are flowers lining the edges and even a few delicate birds drawn here and there. They're pretty but rough, so I think these were just drafts.

Join J. B. and Annette in celebrating the arrival of summer at their new home, Woodmoor, on June twenty-fifth at five thirty in the evening.

June twenty-fifth is in two weeks. I lay all the papers out on my bed, imagining Annette sitting in this very room, planning the party she was so excited about. I bet she even had the song playing in the background. It's so sad that she never got to put that ball gown on again. I swallow through the thickness in my throat.

Glancing back down at the stark, black text, I notice the letters are weird and blocky. They're not a font I easily recognize. Unless...

I snatch up the list, then run to the sunroom and flick on the light. The typewriter is sitting on the table. I hold up the list I just found so I can compare it to the warning message. The letters from the list and the warning message are identical; same size, same color, and same blocky-looking font. Whoa. This means that the new pages I just found in the box were definitely created on a typewriter. Makes sense since they didn't have computers back in the thirties.

Suddenly I'm thinking about Mrs. Sheldon, the owner of the antique shop. She told me and Will that she'd never seen this typewriter before. It was like it just *appeared* the day I arrived and chose Annette's room as my own. I run a finger over the smooth metal, a theory drifting around in my mind.

No, it's not possible. *Is it?*

Gently, I lift the typewriter and look underneath it for evidence. A date, or even a clue about where the typewriter was purchased. It isn't until I search the back panel that I see what I'm looking for. Three small letters engraved into the metal.

A.E.D.

CHAPTER FORTY-THREE

A hiss of air escapes me. This typewriter belonged to Annette Dottinger!

That means every clue I have left leads back to her and the party she wanted to host. The song. The key and the papers in the box. The typewriter. It's as if she's trying to tell me something about that party.

I stare at the warning messages on the typewriter paper, stumped. Like Will said, the first one was pretty clear: *get out.* Annette obviously wanted us to leave, just like she's wanted everyone else to leave. No matter how I look at it, that doesn't seem like it's related to the party.

The second message isn't as simple: *poorhomeallbent.*

I thought I understood this one, but was I wrong? I think back to the moment it showed up. Leo and I were in the ballroom. The typewriter started clicking. We ran downstairs and found this clue. A few seconds later, the tree limb crashed through the ballroom window. The timing made it seem like the message and Mom's smashed kitchen supplies were connected. Now I'm not so sure.

Grabbing my notebook, I sit down on the couch and write *poor home all bent*. I stare at the words, an idea forming in my tired brain. What if this message is like the ticking sound? At first, I thought it was just ticking, like a really loud clock somewhere in the house. It wasn't until I really listened hard that I heard the song behind it. Could this be the same? A clue inside of a clue? The idea is both frightening and exciting. Maybe if I rearrange the words...

Poor bent home all.

Home bent all poor.

Leo *did* read that Mr. Dottinger made some bad business decisions and lost a lot of money, so the "all poor" could make sense. Still, it's not the right kind of clue. It doesn't tell me what to do, like *get out* did.

I give up on trying to rearrange the words and instead focus on the individual letters. Maybe they could be moved around to spell out something else? Something more meaningful? A lot of authors use anagrams in their mysteries.

poorhomeallbent

I start by writing out the words I can create. There are a *lot*. You wouldn't think you could make that many words out of just fifteen letters, but you can. When my list gets long enough to run onto a second sheet of paper, I begin crossing out the words that don't fit. Like *ramen*. I laugh, thinking that Annette Dottinger's urgent message probably doesn't have anything to do with ramen. If the message were coming from someone like my brother, though, I'd totally leave it on the list. Leo's stomach really does take over sometimes.

When I only have words left that aren't too silly, I start rearranging them. It's hard because every time I make a word, I have to cross out every letter I use in my original list so I don't accidentally use it twice.

Room. Open. Not. The. Leap. Or. Ten. Team. Men. Mope. Map. Hot. Ball.

The list feels endless. I rub at my tired eyes, wishing I were better at anagrams. Taking out a few more words, I stare at what I have left. A lot of the words just don't go together, not in a way that makes sense anyway. My eyes skip back and forth between the words *room* and *ball*. I reverse them in my head.

Ball. Room.

Ballroom. The ballroom was important to Annette Dottinger! I excitedly cross those eight letters off in my original list, then look at the remaining ones to see what words I can make.

p̶o̶o̶r̶h̶o̶m̶e̶a̶l̶l̶b̶ent

Within minutes, I have it. A three-word message that sends a full body chill through me.

Open the ballroom.

I burst into Leo's room. He's down on all fours, looking under his bed. He pops up, puts a hand to his chest, and glares at me.

"Gah! Gin, you scared me."

I wave the message in the air between us. "I think I figured out what Annette Dottinger wants."

He stands up and lifts an eyebrow. "She wants us to leave."

"No, look at this." I hold the paper out to him.

"Open the ballroom," Leo says aloud. "Where did you get this?"

"From her last message. It was an anagram. That's why it was worded so weird."

He shakes his head. "Okay, but this doesn't make any sense. Why would Annette's first message be normal and the second be an anagram?"

"I haven't figured that out yet," I admit.

"Also, the ballroom is already open. We were just up there with Will, remember?"

"I know," I sink down to the bed. "But what if she means *open* in a different way? Like, not just unlocked. Annette was the one who wanted to host parties, right?"

"Right," he says hesitantly, like he's not sure where I'm going with this.

"And even though the ballroom isn't exactly locked up, it's not being used. It's just sitting there gathering dust," I continue. "Doesn't that seem like exactly what she *wouldn't* have wanted?"

Annette had big plans for that ballroom. She was going to make it joyful, with music and appetizers and flowers and a band. Until her life was cut short, that is. Now the entire house is the total opposite of joyful. It's dark and bleak. Everything it seems Annette Dottinger would have hated.

Leo looks at the message a second time. "So, what exactly do you think she wants us to do about that?"

The shadows I saw in the ballroom surface in my mind. They were gliding from one side of the room to the other at the same time. Synchronized, almost. Now that I replay it in my mind, it seems possible they weren't just moving but *dancing*. Could Annette have been giving me one of the biggest hints of all that night?

"I think she wants us to host her party." When he doesn't respond, my hope fizzles. I bite the inside of my cheek, wishing I'd kept the thought to myself just a little longer. "Never mind. Maybe it's a dumb idea."

"Wait, you mean 'The Good Old Summertime' party?" There's something about the expression on his face that makes me feel less silly for suggesting it.

"Yeah. What if her spirit has been wandering these halls, trapped here all these years because that was the one big thing she wanted to experience before she," I pause. "Died?"

I fan the other papers out in the air in front of him. "These are her notes for the party. I found them under my bed." Looking down at her sketch of the ballroom, I sigh. "Annette didn't just scribble out some ideas. She planned the whole thing, Leo. She even drew a map of where the tables were going to go. This was obviously really important to her."

Leo looks me straight the eyes. "I don't think this is dumb, Ginny. I think it's brilliant."

Now it's my jaw that drops. I've never heard Leo say the word *brilliant*. And I've definitely never heard him say it about me. "Really?"

"*Really*. I was looking for the ghost books when you came in because I thought there might be clues in them that we missed, something to help us figure out what Annette wants so we can stop the haunting. I should've known you were already ahead of me. You usually are."

I can't keep the smile off my face. Leo and I don't compliment each other very often. It's not that we don't care. We do. It's just that sometimes it's easier to ignore each other than it is to try to get along. I realize now that saying nice things to each other isn't half bad.

"Well, you *did* start all this with your research. That was pretty great, by the way. I thought the ghost books Will brought were going to be super unhelpful, but I was wrong."

Leo looks pleased with himself. I clear my throat, then continue. "Anyway, I borrowed this book while you were in the shower. Thanks, by the way. You were starting to smell like an old gym sock." I decide to tack this on, so things don't get *too* mushy.

He sticks his tongue out at me. Still, he's smiling. Good.

"This might be why the last message was an anagram,

by the way. You like to figure things out. You like mysteries. Maybe Annette decided to use an anagram because she knew you wouldn't quit trying to solve it."

Whoa. I never considered that possibility, but it's cool. Agatha Christie was a master at hooking her readers and keeping them sucked in while the mystery unfolds. Apparently, the ghost of Annette Dottinger is good at it too.

Spreading all the papers out on his comforter, I tap on the party to-do list that Annette was working on. "If we're right, then this is her *motive*—her reason for haunting us. In Agatha's books, every murderer has a reason for killing. Annette's motive for haunting this house is to finally get what she has been waiting for all this time. The party."

Leo gasps. "Remember that conversation Mom and Dad were having?"

I nod. It made me feel bad, like I was failing at solving this mystery and because of that, Dad would fail too. That was the day I realized I can't just run away from a problem, and not just because Agatha wouldn't, but because running away wouldn't fix it.

"Dad was upset about the people around here not liking Woodmoor." My brother paces back and forth, his bare feet gently slapping against the wood. "If the party is Annette's motive, then we have to give it to her, right?"

"Right," I agree, silently impressed with the fact that he used the word *motive*.

"We could... What's that saying about birds and rocks?" he pauses, looking up at the ceiling as if trying to remember something important. "Kill two birds with one stone! That's the saying, right? Once we convince Dad to let us use the ballroom for the party, he can invite people from town to it and show them his plans for the new Woodmoor! Maybe it would get them excited, you know?"

"Yes!" I say. "The party could make Annette happy *and* help Dad!"

Adrenaline is pumping through me now. I feel good. Really good. It's almost better than the feeling I get when I figure out one of Agatha's mysteries before the detective does. Not that that happens very often. Her mysteries are hard to solve.

"It might save us," Leo says.

"And Dad's job," I add.

"And Woodmoor," we say in unison. I look at Leo and he looks at me. Even though neither of us are saying it out loud, I know what we're both thinking. When did we start caring about Woodmoor? About this house that has ruined our summer? Truth is, I don't know. All I know is that Annette Dottinger was excited about this place, that party, maybe even more excited than I was for the writing workshop, and it's not fair that she lost her dreams forever.

It's time somebody gave those dreams back to her.

CHAPTER FORTY-FOUR

Two Weeks Later

I'm fixing the flower centerpieces on the tables for the millionth time when Leo skids to a stop beside me. His tie is crooked, and his hair is sticking out at crazy angles. I smother a laugh with my hand. He's trying.

"Dad said people could start showing up in less than an hour! There's still so much left to do."

"Relax. Mom said she'll be ready to put appetizers out right on time, and the band is setting up now." I hand him a stack of leaflets. "You're still up for greeting, right?"

He looks down at the flyers and nods. They were our idea. Every guest at "The Good Old Summertime" party will be handed one when they come in, and every flyer has a full color floor plan of what Woodmoor will look like one year from today. Dad's plan.

I walk over to the main table where we've displayed all the pictures we found. The one of Annette holding the floor plan is front and center. I smile. We did the impossible; we solved the mystery of Woodmoor Manor. Annette hasn't done anything scary since the day we proposed this party to Mom and Dad. No flickering lights. No locked doors or moving mannequins. No music or whispers from the speaking tube. I think it's because she knew; she knew we were trying to fix this for her, and no one else had done that before.

The mannequin wearing the ball gown is propped up in the corner, the sequins casting glimmering flecks of light on the wood floor. The photo of Annette at the one gathering she got to attend is affixed to the wall next to it. We decided to put it there so people can see how important this ballroom was to her.

Hopefully they see it can be special again. With Dad's plan, Woodmoor can be what she wanted—a beautiful house where people can make memories. I suck in a breath and try to ignore the fluttering in my stomach. It's not fear this time. It's excitement. Even though I'm missing my writing workshop, this has been worth it. I didn't just curl up and read another Agatha Christie novel, I lived one.

The door creaks open, revealing Will. Like Leo, he's

dressed in khaki pants and a button-down shirt. His smile is broad, and his eyes are twinkling. Also, his tie is straight. I'm not surprised.

Walking over, he looks me up and down.

"Wow. You look great, Ginny."

My cheeks heat up. I nervously smooth down the front of my flowery sundress and say thank you. I could tell myself I wore this outfit because it fits the theme of the party, but that would be a lie. I wore it because I think it makes me look pretty, and I knew Will would be here.

A shy smile warms his expression. He extends a hand to reveal a leather-bound book. "I hope this turned out okay. It's not *exactly* the kind of bookmaking I want to do, but it was still fun."

I take it from his hands, marveling at how awesome it looks. I was expecting a notebook with pictures glued into it, not this. It's heavy, like a real book someone would buy in a store. A black-and-white photo of Woodmoor is featured on the cover. I flip through the pages, my own smile growing.

The photos the historical society gave us come up first, J. B. and Annette standing in front of Woodmoor just after it was finished. Then there's pictures of the inside. Gleaming hardwood floors, elegant furniture... It really was beautiful. The last few pages aren't pictures, but a mash-up of different things. Will took all of Annette's ideas—the list, the floor plan, and even a copy of the lyrics to "In the Good Old Summertime"—and turned them into a collage. It takes up two full pages.

Wow.

"Do you like it?" he asks.

I open my mouth to answer, but Leo slaps him on the back before I can speak. "Dude! It's awesome!"

It isn't just awesome; it's thoughtful. Elegant. A perfect way to show how much Annette loved Woodmoor and how much this whole town could love it again if they tried.

"It's perfect," I whisper. What I want to say is that it's just like Will. *He's* thoughtful.

Leo snatches the book from my hands and plops it down in the center of the table.

Mom's heels echo through the room as she walks in. She's only wearing one apron this time, and it doesn't say something funny on it. It has the logo for Dad's company on the front, instead. A whiff of something good hits my nose.

"What is that?" I ask, peering over the edge of the big silver tray in her hands. Mom has been baking for days to prepare for this. She's tried so many different recipes I lost count.

"Appetizers! I have an assortment of nineteen thirties

party food here." She begins pointing at the different plates on her tray. "Pineapple-ginger shrimp cocktail, veal loaf, stuffed tomatoes, and deviled eggs. There's bundt cake coming too!"

I try to snag a piece of shrimp, but she playfully slaps my hand away.

"For the guests. Your guests. Remember?" She winks at me, then pulls a small plastic bag out of her pocket. "I may have made some cookies on the side. Just a few extras for our dedicated staff."

Taking the cookies, I give her a quick hug.

Dad slides up beside her. Unlike when we first got here, he doesn't seem anxious. He seems hopeful. I'm relieved, because when we first told Dad our idea, he was confused.

"A party?" he'd asked, his bushy eyebrows scrunched up. "Could we just back up a second here because I'm lost."

"Leo and I found these notes in my room. They belonged to Annette Dottinger. Remember the party Robert talked about? The 'Good Old Summertime' one? Since she died before it could happen, we were thinking we could host it for her now."

And that's when it happened. Dad's expression had changed. Suddenly he wasn't confused; he was surprised. "I knew that even without the internet you'd figure it out."

"Figure what out?" I asked carefully.

Dad sighed. "That you chose Annette Dottinger's room."

That explained the look on his face when I chose my room. He might not have known all the tragic details or that Annette had been haunting Woodmoor all these years, but he knew the bedroom I chose had a history. A dark one.

"Are you upset with me?" he'd pressed. "I would have told you, but you were already so upset with me for dragging you here that I didn't want to take away the nice room too."

"No, I'm not upset," I said, shocked to discover it was the truth. Annette probably would have haunted us no matter what room I picked. Plus, even though it sounds weird, I'm glad I got wrapped up in this mystery. All these years Annette has watched people come and go, but no one has taken the time to listen, *truly listen*, to her. "I'm just glad there's a happy ending to this story. Plus, I guess I have let my imagination get the better of me before. Once or twice. I don't blame you for not wanting to tell me about Annette's room."

"Ahh, yes. That too." Dad had smiled as his eyes bounced between me and Leo. "So, is this party idea why you two have been acting so strange lately? Playing that record during my meeting? Prowling around at night? *Getting along?*"

"Not really," I answered, just as Leo said, "Totally." We looked at each other and laughed.

"We sort of overheard your conversation with Mom. The

one about how the town wouldn't mind if this place got torn down. This could change their minds." I said this as earnestly as I could. Truth is, I had plenty of evidence to prove the ghost stuff to Dad, but I didn't want to tell him about it anymore. I didn't need to.

Dad clamps a hand down on my shoulder and gently squeezes, jolting me out of my memories. "This looks incredible, everyone. Thanks to you all, I think we have a chance to convince folks that Woodmoor Manor can be special again. Think we're ready to open the floodgates?"

"Almost," Leo answers. "Just one last thing."

With this he rushes to the corner of the room where we've set up the gramophone. He turns it on and gently lowers the needle like he's been practicing. "In the Good Old Summertime" starts playing. Mom dims the lights.

And the room comes to life.

My breath is stolen away by how perfect it looks. The twinkle lights we strung from the ceiling. The banner that reads *Good Old Summertime at Woodmoor*. The flowers with flickering candles on every table.

I don't know if it feels as magical to everyone else as it does to me, but based on their expressions, I think it might. Out of instinct, my eyes glide to the corner—the one where almost all the Shadow People legends started. Will had the idea to turn that area into a photo spot, so we put a wooden bench from the garden there. With delicate white flowers draped along the back and a potted rose bush beside it, there's a new vibe to it now. A peaceful one. Just before I walk away, something catches my eye.

Light. It starts out small, nothing but a pinprick. Slowly, it brightens. Expands. Within seconds, it has taken on a form. The shimmering edges drift across the bench and hover. I stare at it in shock. This is nothing like the shadow I saw before. There are no gnarled arms, no piercing red eyes, no gaping mouth. It's beautiful.

I spin around, my heart thudding. "Will!"

Will is bent down tying his shoe. When he finally stands and follows the line of my trembling finger to the corner, the light is gone.

"What?" Will asks. "Is something wrong with the photo area?"

Shaking my head, I swallow back my shock. The light vanished, but the warm, happy feeling hasn't. I can't prove it, but I know... I just know it was her. *Annette.*

"Ginny?" Will says again, shaking me gently. "Is everything okay?"

I tear my eyes off the bench and smile. Tears prick at my eyelids. Things are better than okay. "Yeah. Everything is great, actually."

From the doorway, Leo begins jumping up and down. He's waving his hands in the air so wildly he looks like a bird about to take off. I laugh, then look at Will who is already wearing his bookstore smile. "I guess that means people are starting to arrive."

"Now might be a good time to mention that someone special is coming tonight," he says.

I look at him sideways. "Who? Your boss?"

He smiles. "Nope."

"Your parents?"

"Wrong again." Will laughs.

I'm about to give him a good shake and hope the answer falls out when the door opens. A familiar boy, with familiar blue eyes, walks in and waves. *Craig.*

I never thought Craig would want to come here again. Not after what happened to him. "I can't believe it."

Will shrugs. "His idea, not mine."

I'm still in shock when Craig reaches us. "Hey, hi. I mean, wow. You came."

"I did," he says, casting a suspicious look into the corner. "I had to see if it was true."

"If what was true?"

"That you fixed this place." He surveys the decorations and nods slowly. "Will has been talking about your plan

293

for weeks. Kept telling me you finally figured out how to make Woodmoor normal again. I guess I wanted to see it for myself."

"Did I succeed?" I ask.

"Yeah, I think you did," he says with a grin. "Now maybe I won't hate coming here every summer. Even being in the same town as this place freaked me out. It feels different now. Better."

I lean in close so none of the other guests can hear me. "She's happy now."

He purses his lips together, then exhales. "Good. Because I didn't like her when she was angry."

A laugh escapes me. Then another. Before I know it, we're all cracking up. Without warning, Will slides his hand into mine for the second time since I came to Michigan. I freeze, afraid that if I move he'll take it back.

He doesn't.

EPILOGUE

"That's it!" Dad says, setting the last of our suitcases into the trunk and closing it. It's close to the end of July, and there's no hint of the storms we lived through for most of June. Only sun. Hot, welcoming Michigan sun. "Maybe we can get on the road soon?"

"Sounds good." I check my pockets for my ear buds, convinced I won't survive the drive back to Chicago without them. Not with my brother blabbering on next to me, anyway. Apparently, Leo has decided that video games are out, and paranormal activity is in. He's been reading anything and everything he can get his hands on about hauntings both here and in Chicago. He even found out about this ghost tour called Spirits of Chicago that he swears he's going to take as soon as we get back home. Of course, Will loves it. He's shown up at the house with arms full of books more times than I can count.

I laugh, thinking that Annette Dottinger did more than just inspire my newest short story. She turned my brother into a reader. A *nerd*.

Dad heads back into the house where Mom is checking each room one at a time to make sure we haven't left anything. I swear, if she asks me again if I have all of my charging cords, I'm going to scream.

I'm watching the driveway when he pulls up. Will. His father stops and lets him out before pulling into one of the farthest spots and turning off the engine.

"Hey," he says, shielding his eyes from the sun.

"Hey," I answer back. The ache in my stomach starts up again. It's the one that I get every time I think about leaving here and not seeing Will again. He's not my boyfriend or anything, but he's still special. Still someone I want to hang out with more.

He looks up at Woodmoor. The sun is sparkling off the windows, and the new flowers lining the sidewalk sway in the gentle breeze. Even the grass is greener, thick and emerald colored instead of crunchy and brown. It feels so different from the day I arrived here that it's hard to believe this is the same place.

"You all packed up?"

"Yeah. We're supposed to leave soon." I dig the toe of my sandal into the gravel. This is worse than the day I did the awkward shoulder pat. There are so many things I want to say to Will, but they all seem to stay tangled up behind my tongue.

"I wish you didn't have to go."

It's so quiet I almost don't hear it. I jerk my head up to face Will, surprised to see his mouth is tilted down into a frown.

"Me too." I swallow back the sadness I feel building. I knew this day was coming. I guess I just didn't know it would hurt so bad.

"Will," Dad emerges from the house, a handful of cords in his hand. I narrow my eyes on them, wincing when I recognize the one that goes to my computer. I'm never going to hear the end of that. "Nice to see you. Good timing too."

I shoot a confused look at him. Unless he means Will is here just in time to watch me drive away in a cramped minivan, I have no idea what Dad could be talking about.

"Oh, didn't I tell you? I need to come back here for a long weekend in September. You know, consult with some people in the historical society and see how the renovations are going. In fact, I'll probably have to come back here every couple of months for a while. Keep tabs on things."

"You will?" I ask, stunned. This is the first time I've heard this.

"No, *we* will," he corrects. "I wouldn't want to pick out our new vacation home without your input."

"V-v-vaca…" I'm trying to talk, but I guess Will thinks I'm choking because he slaps me on the back. I give him a look. "Vacation home?"

Dad laughs. "Well, if we're going to be here so frequently, we might as well. Unless, of course, you hate the idea."

He says this with a smirk. Dad knows I don't hate the idea. When we first arrived here in Michigan, I would have done anything to crawl back into the car, drive back home, and never see this place again. Now? It's not half bad. I've had a chance to walk through the forest trails too, and this time didn't get run over by a raccoon. I also didn't get snatched up by the Hitchhikers. Maybe nothing lives in the woods, but now that I know I'll be coming back here, I make myself a promise that I'll get to the bottom of that legend.

Huh. I guess I don't want to just write mysteries, after all; I want to *solve* them.

Dad sticks a thumb out toward the house. "I'll just go round up your brother and mom."

He shoves the cords into my hands and walks off, humming "In the Good Old Summertime."

Will smiles. It's so bright it competes with the sun. "Whoa."

"Right?" I say. "I guess this isn't really a goodbye, now. More like a *see you later*."

"An *hasta luego*."

"A..." I pause, realizing I don't know any other way to say *see you later*. "Anyway, my internet isn't sketchy back in Chicago like it is here. Phone works too."

"Cool. I'll call you." He reaches up and pulls a backpack off that I hadn't noticed before. Unzipping it, Will rummages around until he finds what he's after. It's a gift, wrapped in paper with little typewriters on it. He sees me eyeing it and says, "Since you don't get to keep Annette's typewriter."

I grin and take it from his hand. Once I told Dad what I figured out about the typewriter, we decided it would be best to donate it to Robert and the other owners of Woodmoor. As cool as it is, it belongs in the house. Besides, it still creeps me out. Just a *little*.

A horn breaks the silence. Will's dad. A lot of things have changed around here, but his schedule apparently isn't one of them.

"Ugh. I better go. Talk tonight?"

"Totally. Thanks for this." I hold the package in the air.

He chuckles. "Don't thank me yet. For all you know, that could be something really sinister. Like a ransom note. Or a thumb."

"A thumb?" I laugh as he starts to back pedal away from me. I wish I could memorize this moment. The sensation of being on the edge of everything wonderful. It's probably how Annette felt when she saw the floor plans for Woodmoor for the first time.

I watch Will's car pull out of the driveway, waving until it's only a speck in the distance. Then I open the package. It's a book. Not just any book, though, *my* book.

In the Shadows

by

Ginny Anderson

My eyes widen. I can't believe he remembered. Will asked me what I like to write, and I told him a lot of stuff, but that it might be fun to write a short story about Woodmoor. I didn't expect him to do something like this. Most people wouldn't.

Opening the cover, I smile at the sound of the spine cracking and the smell of leather and fresh paper that wafts out. The pages inside are blank, waiting for me to start the story that's been growing in my brain. The story of a forgotten family, a bizarre legend, and a fearful town. It won't be Annette's story, but it will definitely have something in common with her.

Woodmoor.

ACKNOWLEDGMENTS

Leo wisely tells Ginny that her hero, Agatha Christie, did not write all her books alone. This is so, so true. Every successful author owes a great deal of that success to her team, and my team is truly special.

To my family—thank you. Thank you for putting up with me being scattered and occupied while I'm writing. Thank you for hugging me when things are hard and for celebrating with me when there's a victory. I love you all so, so much. You're my inspiration.

To Annie Berger and the entire team at Sourcebooks—thank you. Without all of you and your many gifts/skills, this book would still be trapped inside of my ridiculously cluttered brain.

To my friends and CPs—Jenni Walsh, Becky Wallace, Lynne Matson, Jen Calonita, and Jen Cervantes—thank you!

Without all of you, I'd never have the confidence or stamina to even finish a book. I love you all.

To all of my amazing educator friends—thank you. Your support over the years has meant so much, and I couldn't do this without you. A special shout-out to Steph McHugh and Kate Paulson for going above and beyond to help spread the word about my books. I'm truly grateful.

Last but not least, to my readers—thank you! There would be no books without you. Your enthusiasm motivates me more than you know. I'm grateful to continue writing books for you.

DON'T MISS ANOTHER SPOOKY STORY FROM LINDSAY CURRIE

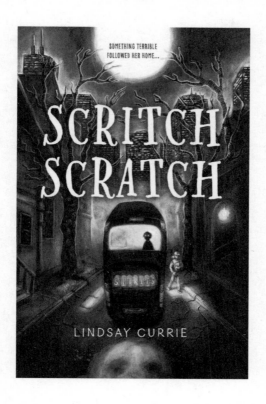

"A teeth-chattering, eyes bulging, shuddering-and-shaking, chills-at-the-back-of-your-neck ghost story. I loved it!"
—R. L. Stine, author of the Goosebumps series

ONE

If someone had told me yesterday that I'd be spending my Saturday morning in the aisle of a stuffy bookstore searching for ghost stories, I would've told them they were nuts. But here I am, staring down an entire row of books with titles like *Windy City Mysteries*, *Chi-Town Haunts*, and *Second City Ghosts*.

I guess I should've expected this. Having a dad who is interested in creepy Chicago history is one thing, but having a dad who is *obsessed* with it is another thing altogether. Two years ago, he wrote a mystery novel called *Spirits of Chicago*. He went on a book tour and even did an interview on the local news station. I was cool with it at first, but when he announced to the family that he was quitting his job teaching history to start a tour bus company, things went sideways. See, it wasn't just any tour bus company. It was a *ghost* tour bus company.

Seriously.

Ghost tours.

So it's no big shocker that we're standing in this bookstore instead of going home. Dad is drawn to this kind of stuff. The dark. The sinister. The *ghostly*.

I prefer beakers and test tubes to gravestones and mausoleums. Science is predictable. Comforting. It's something you can see, hear, touch, and smell—unlike Dad's "ghosts."

"The boulder isn't even placed over Kennison's actual burial site," Dad mutters to no one in particular. This is how he gets when he's researching. It's more like a trance than anything, so usually I just leave him alone. Only today it's hard. This place could put a Mountain Dew addict to sleep.

A giggle breaks the silence. I swivel my head, looking for my best friend, Casley. That was her giggle; I'm sure of it. I start to walk in the direction I *think* the laughter came from, but I stop in my tracks when I realize she isn't alone. Staying behind a bookshelf, I watch Cas flip through the pages of a graphic novel while Emily Craig reads over her shoulder. They burst into laughter more than once, the sound of their happiness needling me. I ease farther behind the bookshelf and force myself to breathe through the ache in my stomach. Cas didn't invite me to hang out with them; she didn't even mention it.

Emily just moved here a couple of months ago, but Casley has been hanging out with her more and more lately. Inviting her to sit at our lunch table, begging her to join the science club, including her on group texts. There's nothing wrong with Emily; I mean, she seems nice enough. But she's quiet when I'm around. Casley swears it's nothing. I'm not so sure. I guess I get it; Emily and I don't have anything in common. She's into stuff Cas and I have never been into before. Makeup. Hair products. Clothes. Now that Casley seems to be into these things too, I feel like I don't belong whenever the three of us are together.

"Dad," I whisper, rounding the corner where my father is still standing, nose in a book. "Can we go now?"

He slowly flips a page, then immediately turns it back as if he might have missed something. I drop my face into my hands and groan. The longer we stay here, the more likely it is that Cas will see me. Even worse, she might think I'm spying on her.

"Dad!" I hiss louder, ignoring the pointed stare of a man shuffling past. "I have to work on my science fair project. Can you just buy the book so we can go home?"

Dad looks up, blinking at me as if he has just remembered I'm here. He probably has.

"Oh. Sure thing, Claire. Let me check out really quick, and I'll get you home."

I scan the aisles nervously, suddenly aware that Casley's laughter has quieted down. Maybe they left. Peeking around the bookshelf at the register, I groan at my bad luck. Not only is Casley still here, she's buying something.

Dad heaves his enormous messenger bag off the floor and taps on the cover of the book he's holding. The picture on the front is of several men in suits smoking cigars and leaning against a brick wall. The word *massacre* is printed across the lower half of the photo in a shocking red that looks like it's dripping down the page.

I wince. "Is that supposed to be blood?"

"It's about a Mob hit in the 1920s where seven men died, so I would assume so," Dad says with a dry chuckle. "I've never considered making the site of the Saint Valentine's Day Massacre part of the tour, but this book might have changed my mind. There's been quite a lot of paranormal activity documented there. Plus, the site is so close. Practically right next to your school!"

Next to my school? My skin bristles uncomfortably. I've learned a lot over the last two years about our neighborhood, Lincoln Park, and unfortunately, it's all bad. Unlike most parents, Dad doesn't focus on *normal* Chicago history when he tells stories. Forget protests and pioneers and famous residents. Instead, it's always some nightmarish tragedy that left behind an angry, restless spirit (or several). Whatever. Dad's stories used to scare me, but that was back before I was into science and knew how fake all this stuff is.

"Ready to hit the road?" He nudges me toward the cashier with a conspiratorial grin, as if I'm just as excited about his new book as he is. Little does he know that I'd rather eat the book than read it.

"Mm-hmm," I mumble, slowly picking my bag up off the floor to waste time. If Dad rushes for the checkout line right now, he'll run straight into Cas. He'll show her the book. He might even start talking about his ghost tours, and even though Casley is used to it, Emily isn't. No matter how nice Casley thinks she is, she'll start rumors. New people always do.

Slinging my bag over my shoulder, I snatch the book from Dad's hands. "You can get this cheaper online."

Dad looks like he's been slapped. "You know I don't like shopping online, Claire! That is driving bookstores like this out of business!"

Darn. If this store goes out of business, it will be one less place for Dad to embarrass us. "I'm just saying that if you want the book, you could get it tomorrow for way less by doing that."

Please listen. Please try to hear what I'm actually saying. Please, please, please.

Dad shoves his glasses up his nose and gives me a stern

look. Reaching over, he pries my fingers off the book one at a time. "The price is fine, Little Miss Cheapskate. Let's go."

Just when I think I have no choice but to trip him or fake an injury of my own to slow him down, I hear the jingle of the small bell above the door. Someone left! Trotting to the window, I exhale in relief. It was Casley. She skips away from the store, one willowy arm linked through Emily's like a fence—a fence meant to keep me out.

ABOUT THE AUTHOR

Lindsay Currie lives in Chicago, Illinois, with her high school sweetheart turned husband and their three amazing children. Although she didn't go to school to be a historian, researching her city's complex and often spooky history is one of Lindsay's favorite things to do—especially when there are ghost legends involved! If you'd like to find out what books Lindsay has coming out next and discover some fun, behind-the-scenes facts about her, like one of her favorite places to vacation (think mouse ears!) or what color hair she's always wanted to have, visit her website at lindsaycurrie.com.